Practice I

by

Jay Northcote

To Lindsay
Thanks for reading!
Love
Jay x

Copyright

Cover artist: Garrett Leigh.
Editor: Sue Adams.
Practice Makes Perfect © 2016 Jay Northcote.

ALL RIGHTS RESERVED

This literary work may not be reproduced or transmitted in any form or by any means, including electronic or photographic reproduction, in whole or in part, without express written permission. This is a work of fiction and any resemblance to persons, living or dead, or business establishments, events or locales is coincidental.
The Licensed Art Material is being used for illustrative purposes only.
All Rights Are Reserved. No part of this may be used or reproduced in any manner whatsoever without written permission, except in the case of brief quotations embodied in critical articles and reviews.

Warning
This book contains material that is intended for a mature, adult audience. It contains graphic language, explicit sexual content, and adult situations.

CHAPTER ONE

"Are you sure you don't need help with anything else?" Rupert asked, surveying the mess of bags, boxes, and black bin liners that contained all of Dev's worldly possessions — apart from the ones that were still in his bedroom back home in Oxford.

"No, honestly, I'm good. Thanks again for helping me move."

Rupert had a car, and he and his boyfriend Josh had insisted on helping Dev move across town from the halls of residence he'd been so glad to escape from. This room in a shared house was his new start for the summer term.

"It was no trouble." Rupert smiled.

"It's so weird to think this used to be my room. It feels like ages ago that I moved out." Josh moved to stand beside Rupert, looking around the room as Rupert slipped his arm around Josh's shoulders.

"Seven months." Rupert kissed Josh's temple, his face full of affection.

Seeing them together made Dev's heart squeeze with longing. Not because he fancied Rupert — although he did have a bit of a crush — but because he wanted what they had.

He wanted a boyfriend.

"I guess we'll leave you to it, then," Rupert said. "Let you get yourself sorted."

"Okay." Dev adjusted his glasses, which were slipping on the bridge of his nose. He was hot and sweaty after several trips up two flights of stairs with heavy bags and boxes. "Thanks again."

Rupert's brow furrowed as he studied Dev. "Hey," he said softly. "You'll be okay here. Shawn can be a bit of a twat sometimes, but the rest of them are good people."

Dev nodded. His stomach was full of butterflies despite Rupert's reassuring words. Dev had briefly met his new housemates when he'd looked around the house a couple of weeks ago, but he didn't really know any of them; he didn't even know Rupert very well. He trusted Rupert's judgement, though. Rupert had been kind when Dev had badly needed a friend, and he'd helped him find this place to live. If Rupert said he'd be okay here, Dev believed him.

"Text me if you need anything, yeah? And we'll see you soon." Rupert stepped forward and drew Dev into a hug. Dev hugged him back a little awkwardly. He wasn't used to physical contact, and although he craved it, Rupert's closeness had him flustered.

"Thanks," Dev mumbled into Rupert's shoulder.

When Rupert released him, Josh gave Dev a hug too, and a light kiss on the cheek. "Take care."

When they'd gone, Dev closed the door behind them. Taking a deep breath, he turned and took stock of his surroundings.

It was utter chaos. Just looking at it made Dev's blood pressure rise. The room was warm and stuffy too. He wrinkled his nose, catching the faint scent of tobacco smoke, along with another, more pungent smell Dev couldn't quite identify. Paul, the previous occupant, had obviously ignored the house rules about not smoking indoors.

Dev opened the window wide, letting in a blast of cool April air, and then perched on the edge of the bed with a notepad and pen. He wrote a list in his neat, precise handwriting.

unpack

go to supermarket (He'd need another list for that.)

eat

phone home

With his list written, Dev was calmer already. Unpacking first, then.

Several hours later, Dev sat on his neatly made bed and picked up his notepad again. He leaned back against the pillows to rest his aching back, and he crossed off *unpack*.

Exhausted, all he wanted to do was chill out for the rest of the day, but he was hungry, and eating involved moving. Having previously lived in student accommodation with catering, or at home with parents who fed him, Dev wasn't used to cooking for himself, but there was a microwave, so he wasn't going to starve. Reluctantly he heaved himself up, put on a hoodie, and put his wallet in his jeans pocket.

Music came from one of the rooms on the floor below as he passed, along with chatter from the living room. Dev wasn't ready to be sociable yet, so he went straight out, escaping to the solitude of the street.

It was a nice evening, mild for early April. The sky was mostly blue with just a few fluffy white clouds. A fresh breeze blew, carrying the scent of city streets and the sea.

A small supermarket was handy, just a short walk away on the main road leading towards the city centre. Obviously used to catering for students, it stocked a load of cheap pizzas and ready meals, plus things in cans, jars, or packets that could be heated up and added to pasta or rice.

Wishing he'd made more effort to learn to cook before leaving home, Dev gathered an assortment of things that looked vaguely edible and easy to prepare.

He was nearly back at his front door when the pounding of feet made him look up to see a guy running towards him, flat out sprinting down the pavement. His bright red hair caught the evening sun, a blaze of glory in the drab city street.

Bags in hand, Dev stepped aside to let the guy past.

The runner pulled up in front of him with a grin. "It's all right. I'm stopping here." He jerked his head at the house next door to Dev's. He was tall and broad-shouldered, and his chest heaved as he breathed hard. Sweat stuck his pale blue running shirt to his skin, showcasing the outline of nice pecs and nipples. Dev quickly snapped his gaze back to the guy's face.

"Oh, me too," Dev said. "I mean… I live here." He raised a bag-laden hand and pointed his thumb at his own front door.

The ginger guy's brow wrinkled with a frown. "I haven't seen you before."

He had a slight accent, Scottish, perhaps? His gaze scanned Dev in a way that made Dev's skin tingle. Something flared in the amber eyes; could it be interest? Dev wasn't used to that kind of attention. He must be imagining it. "Yeah. I just moved in."

"Ah well, we're neighbours, then. I'm Ewan." He stuck out a hand.

Dev fumbled to pass a carrier bag of shopping to his other hand so he could shake. Ewan's hand was big and warm, and he gripped Dev's hand tightly. Dev's heart beat faster and his cheeks heated. Ewan's eyes were warm too, and his smile was infectious.

"I'm Dev. It's good to meet you, Ewan."

As soon as the words came out, Dev cursed himself for sounding so formal. Why couldn't he just say hi like a normal person?

"Dev?" Ewan repeated.

Dev nodded. People often repeated his name to check, no matter how clearly he said it.

Ewan finally released his hand. "I expect I'll see you around then, Dev. Bye." He grabbed one of his ankles and pulled his foot behind him into a quad stretch.

Dev really tried not to look at the pale skin and lean muscles of Ewan's thigh. "Yeah." Belatedly, Dev realised the conversation was over. "Okay, then. I'll just…."

He climbed the couple of steps to his front door, put his bags down, and fumbled with his keys in the lock for a few awkward seconds, convinced Ewan was watching him. But when he looked back, Ewan had dropped forward to stretch his hamstrings. With his back to Dev, the curve of his arse begged to be admired.

"Bye, then," Dev said weakly.

Dev's heart tripped faster for a different reason as he closed the front door behind him. Noises drifted from the kitchen. It was time to face his new housemates—or some of them, at least.

Although he'd met them all when he looked around the house a couple of weeks ago, Dev wasn't sure he could remember their names.

Three guys worked side by side in the small kitchen. A stocky, sandy-haired bloke stood over a sandwich toaster; a tall guy with cropped dark hair stirred something in a pan; and a third with messy, dirty-blond hair, sat on the worktop near the cooker, with a beer in his hand.

"Um, hi," Dev said as he walked in.

The blond guy on the counter grinned. "Hi, Dev. It *is* Dev, isn't it? Not Des?"

The other blokes both looked up and nodded in greeting.

"Yeah, it's Dev. Devrim, actually, but everyone calls me Dev. Sorry... can you remind me of your names again?"

"Sure. I'm Jez," the blond, obviously the chatty one of the group, said. "And this is Mac,"—he indicated the tall guy who was cooking—"and Shawn."

Shawn didn't respond to the introduction, but Mac smiled. "Welcome to the madhouse."

"Thanks." Dev managed a shy smile back. He raised his shopping bags. "So... is there a particular cupboard for me or something?"

"Yeah. Let me show you." Jez hopped down. He opened a cupboard over the microwave. "This one's empty now, and in the fridge, the second shelf down is yours." He opened the fridge. "Well it should be yours, but our stuff has spread to fill the space since Paul left. Hang on." He moved a few things around. "There you go."

"Thanks." Dev was grateful for Jez's cheerful chatter. Socially awkward, Dev was crap at keeping conversations going. It was always a relief when someone else did it for him.

"So, are you all settled in?" Jez asked as Dev put his few things in the fridge.

"Yeah, I think so."

Shawn spoke next, and his tone was oddly accusing as he asked, "So, how come you moved out of halls partway through the year? You're a first year, yes?"

Dev tensed. Avoiding Shawn's curious gaze, he moved to the cupboard and started to stack stuff on the shelf. "Yeah. I, um… it just didn't really work out very well, so I wanted a change."

There was a short, uncomfortable silence. Dev was painfully aware of them absorbing his words. He might as well have just slapped a big sign on his head that read "Victim." With his skinny frame, thick glasses, and slightly odd mannerisms, Dev had been a walking target for bullies when he was younger. But in his later years at school, he'd found his niche with weird, geeky gamers like himself, so he'd become complacent.

If he'd ended up sharing a corridor with guys like that at uni, he'd have been fine, but unfortunately for him, he'd been landed with a group of macho dickheads who made his life a misery. Dev had assumed Rupert would fill in his new housemates on the mess that was his life at uni so far, but apparently not.

Mac was the one to break the silence. "Well, I guess it was lucky for you that Paul dropped out, then." His voice was kind and genuine, and when Dev dared to turn around and face him, there was sympathy in his eyes.

"Yeah." Dev tried to lean nonchalantly against the counter, but succeeded in being about as nonchalant as a plank of wood. He wanted to escape to his room, but he was hungry. He wondered where the pans were kept. "How come Paul left? Rupert never said."

"He got kicked out," Jez said. "He was a nice guy, but a total stoner. I don't think he made it to any lectures, ever. He was high 24/7 unless he was sleeping."

That explained the funny smell in Dev's room.

"How do you know Rupert, anyway?" Shawn's gaze stayed fixed on Dev.

Dev's cheeks heated at the inquisition. What the hell was the guy's problem with him? "I work part-time in the IT support team. I don't know him that well, but one day we got talking, and I told him about… I mentioned the, um, issues I was having. And he knew about the room going here."

Shawn grunted in acknowledgement and turned back to the toasted-sandwich maker. It sizzled as he opened it, and Shawn slid the sandwich onto his waiting plate. He picked it up and left the room without another word.

Dev relaxed as soon as Shawn had gone, his hackles lowering and muscles unbunching from the fight-or-flight response that Shawn's aggressive questioning had triggered.

"Ignore him," Jez said. "He's just being a dick because he and Mike wanted to move one of their mates in, but they were outvoted. Me, Mac, and Dani wanted you instead."

"Oh." Dev swallowed, a little overwhelmed by the admission. "Well, thanks."

"Rupert didn't tell Shawn and Mike why you needed the room, but he told the rest of us, and it's cool. You can be yourself here. Don't worry about Shawn. He'll get over himself eventually. If he managed to get used to me and Mac snogging on the sofa, he'll get used to living with you too."

"Oh, so you two are...?" Dev wasn't sure how to end that sentence.

Shagging. A couple. Together?

Jez grinned, his face lighting up as he glanced sideways at Mac. "Yeah, we're boyfriends. We've been together over a year now."

Mac sidled closer to Jez and put an arm around his shoulders.

"Oh." Dev gave a tentative smile. "Rupert mentioned that two of the guys in the house were gay, but he didn't say you were a couple."

Mac frowned then. "We're not gay. We're bi. But whatever."

"Oh, sorry."

"That's okay. Rupert should know better," Jez said. "We've explained it to him enough times. He's just lazy."

"I'm gay." Dev's stomach dropped as nerves swooped through him. He'd only said those words out loud to a few people before: his parents and his best mates at school. "I mean, it's cool that you're bi, but I'm definitely gay."

"Have you ever... with a girl?" Jez asked.

Dev's face burned as he shook his head. "No." He wasn't admitting he'd never done anything with a boy either. But he knew he was gay. He'd known since he was ten years old. All his fantasies starred guys, and flat chests, and dicks. "But I know enough to know that I don't want to."

The timer on the cooker beeped, and Mac turned back to the stove. He took a lid off, releasing a cloud of steam. "I think this spaghetti's done," he said to Jez. "Get some plates out?"

Dev watched enviously as Mac dished up something that looked like bolognese. It smelled really good. When Mac was done, he left the pans by the sink.

"We'll get out of your way now," Jez said. "It's good to finally meet you properly, Dev."

"Yeah, you too."

Left alone in the kitchen, Dev opened his food cupboard again and surveyed the contents. "Pasta and sauce it is, I guess," he muttered.

After rummaging around in the other cupboards, Dev managed to find a couple of clean saucepans. He poured pasta into one, guessing the quantity, and emptied a jar of sauce into the other. It fell out with a distinctly unappetising *splat*. Dev poked it suspiciously.

Whatever Mac cooked had looked a lot nicer. He'd better add *learn to cook* to his longer-term list of things to do.

Sitting on his bed, Dev yawned, his full stomach making him sleepy. He stared at his phone as he contemplated calling home but decided he couldn't face it tonight. He loved his mum, but she did tend to bang on. Once she got him on the line, she'd end up talking for ages and asking him a million questions he was too tired to answer. Instead, he sent his mum a quick text.

All moved in, everything's good. I'm shattered now so I'm going to have an early night. I'll call you tomorrow.

She replied within seconds as though she'd been waiting for him to call.

Okay sweetie, glad you're settled. Sleep well xxx

He picked up his notepad and crossed off *phone home*. Texting counted. He also crossed off everything else on his list for today. That was Saturday done.

Dev set his notepad aside, opened his laptop, and pulled up his lists app. He liked his notepad for day-to-day organisation; it gave him a certain satisfaction to cross out the things he'd done and to get to the end of the day with all the tasks completed. But for longer-term planning, he kept his lists on his Mac, synced to his phone.

For the first time in six months, Dev could breathe again. Finally he had a safe place where he could get back on track and look to the future. He began to type.

Things To Do This Term
Make some friends
Learn to cook
Research sex stuff
Join Grindr
Get some experience
Find a boyfriend

He stared at the words on the screen and sighed. That seemed like a lot of things to aim for. But it was good to have goals, right? Jez and Mac seemed really nice, so hopefully Dev was already on his way to achieving the first objective. And that bloke Ewan… Dev's mind conjured up the image of the flame-haired hunk who lived next door. Ewan had been friendly.

Maybe there was potential there too.

CHAPTER TWO

Ewan happened to be in when the Amazon delivery guy arrived.

He signed for the package and carried it into the kitchen. He was expecting the new bike lights he'd ordered, and it was rare for anyone else in the house to order anything online. They were all skint students. So it was perfectly reasonable for him to open the package without checking the name on the front first.

Ewan was alone, back from an early-afternoon lecture, and he tore into the cardboard packaging as he waited for the kettle to boil for his Pot Noodle. He stared down at the contents of the box.

"What the fuck?" he muttered.

A hot flush crawled up his neck and over his face. That definitely wasn't a bike light.

It was a dildo. A very nice-looking dildo, if you were into that sort of thing — and Ewan was. This one looked expensive, much classier than the cheap, tacky one Ewan had. The new dildo was smallish but perfectly formed, an attractive shade of dark blue with a realistic cockhead and some subtle veins on the shaft. A curved handle meant it would be good for solo use.

Ewan wondered which of his flatmates was going to kill him for opening it by mistake. His money was on Nadia because the other guys in the house were relentlessly straight as far as he was aware. He couldn't imagine any of them sticking anything up their arses. Unless... Ryan, maybe? He was the adventurous type. But Nadia seemed the most likely candidate. Justine was pretty sheltered... but then again, sometimes the quiet ones surprised you.

He turned the package over to look at the label and frowned. On the box he read a name he didn't recognise: Devrim Karadere — maybe someone who'd lived in the house last year? But then Ewan looked more carefully and realised the package shouldn't have come to their house. It was supposed to have been delivered next door.

"Devrim," Ewan muttered. "Devrim... *Dev*." The pieces slotted into place.

The intended recipient of the dildo was obviously the cute guy who'd moved in next door last weekend. Since their encounter in the street, Ewan had seen him coming and going a few times. They'd exchanged greetings but nothing more.

Dev seemed shy, but he always smiled at Ewan, and something about that smile and those dark Bambi eyes behind his thick-framed glasses made Ewan's stomach flutter.

He'd been wondering whether Dev was gay, and he supposed the dildo answered his question. Okay, some straight guys liked anal play, but not usually with anything shaped like a real dick.

The sound of the front door and voices in the hallway startled Ewan out of his reverie. He closed the package quickly and stuck it under his arm. Abandoning his Pot Noodle, he hurried out.

Passing Ryan and James on his way to the stairs, he muttered a hurried greeting without stopping to chat.

In his room, Ewan studied the package again, wondering whether he could tape it up in such a way that it wasn't obvious he'd opened it. But there was no way that would work. It was one of those with the cardboard strip you had to tear out to open. He could stick the package shut, but it would be clear it had been tampered with.

For a wild moment, he considered keeping the bloody thing. He could have some fun with it… and then Dev would presumably tell Amazon it had never arrived, so they'd send him a replacement. But no, that wouldn't work either because he'd signed for the bloody thing.

There was nothing else for it. He'd just have to tape it up and deliver it next door himself.

Ewan stood on the doorstep of the house next door, his heart pounding hard.

It's no big deal. It's only a dildo. It was an honest mistake.

Maybe if nobody was in he could just leave it on the doorstep….

He rang the doorbell, anxiety spiking higher as he heard footsteps on the stairs.

If Dev was out, he could leave it with one of the other housemates. That would probably be less embarrassing all round. But he really ought to explain what had happened.

A tall bloke with cropped dark hair opened the door. He gave Ewan a friendly smile. "Oh, hi. Ewan, isn't it?"

He was called Mick or Max or something, Ewan couldn't remember. Ewan and his housemates had had a party at the start of the year, and the people next door had shown up for a while, but a lot of alcohol had been involved. Since then, they'd always said hi in passing but hadn't really spoken.

"Yeah. Hi… uh, Max, was it? Sorry, I'm shit with names."

"Mac."

Ewan shuffled his feet and gripped the package more tightly. Dump it and run, or fess up? If he'd ordered a sex toy and someone next door had opened it, he might freak out a little. He wanted to reassure Dev that his secret was safe—if it was a secret. Maybe Dev was out and proud and didn't give a shit who knew about his sex toys.

Ewan decided it was better to be honest.

"Did you want something in particular?" Mac asked.

Ewan realised he'd been standing there in silence like an idiot while his brain worked through the best way to deal with the situation. "Um, yeah, sorry. Is Dev in?"

"I think so. Come in." Mac turned, obviously expecting Ewan to follow him.

Ewan shut the door behind him and walked up the stairs behind Mac. This house was identical in layout to the one next door.

On the first landing, Mac stopped at the bottom of the stairs that led up to the top floor. "Dev?" he yelled. "You in, mate?"

"Yes" came the faint answer from above.

"You've got a visitor." Mac bellowed, then spoke more quietly to Ewan. "Go on up."

Ewan hesitated. That wasn't what he'd envisaged. He'd hoped to thrust the package at Dev, mutter an apology for opening it, and leave. But now he had to go and invade the poor guy's room. Maybe he should have given it to Mac and fled, but it was too late now.

He climbed the stairs, and when he rounded the corner at the top, came face to face with a surprised-looking Dev standing in the doorway to his room. Dev was dressed in jeans and a T-shirt, but his feet were bare. His dark hair was rumpled as though he'd been running his hands through it. He blinked at Ewan in surprise through his thick-framed glasses.

"Hi," Ewan said.

"Oh. It's you." Dev met his gaze and his cheeks flushed.

"Ewan."

Dev's blush deepened. "I remember. Hi." His gaze dropped to the box in Ewan's hands.

Ewan's fingers curled more tightly around the package. "Um, this is a little awkward. Can I come in?"

No way was he having this conversation out on the landing.

Dev raised his eyebrows. "Sure." He turned and walked into his room.

Ewan followed, closing the door behind him.

Dev's room was an advertisement for how student accommodation was supposed to look, but never did in Ewan's experience. From the perfectly organised shelves to the tidy desk and gleaming laptop, nothing was out of place. Dev even had an actual laundry basket rather than the ubiquitous pile of dirty clothes in the corner.

"So, um, what did you want?" Dev asked.

Ewan braced himself. Now he was the one blushing. "Yeah, this is awkward." He held out the package to Dev. "I'm really sorry, but they delivered this next door by mistake, and I was expecting my new bike lights that I'd ordered from Amazon, so I opened it without checking the name. And, uh… it wasn't my bike lights. It's actually something for you."

He winced, forcing himself to meet Dev's gaze.

Confusion showed on Dev's features at first, and then a dawning horror. Ewan expected embarrassment, but instead of turning red again, the colour drained from Dev's olive skin, leaving him pale, with tension in every line of his slender frame. Dev glanced over Ewan's shoulder at the closed door as though looking for an escape route.

There was a horrible, painful silence.

Ewan was still holding the package out, but Dev didn't take it. He was staring at the package as though it was a bomb, or a severed hand or something.

"It's okay," Ewan said.

Dev was obviously incapable of speaking, so it was up to Ewan to salvage the situation, which had spiralled into something far more hideous than he had been expecting.

"Seriously, mate. Don't freak out. It's only a dildo. I know it's embarrassing, but it's nothing to be ashamed of."

Dev still didn't reply, but his gaze crept back up to Ewan's face. He frowned, studying Ewan carefully as though trying to work out whether Ewan was genuine or not.

"Honestly. I'm really sorry," Ewan continued, desperate to reassure him. "And it's totally cool… it's actually a really nice dildo. Kudos on an excellent choice. It looks classy. Mine stinks of cheap chemicals and it's bright pink, but it was on special offer, so…."

Dev's lips quirked in an unexpected smile and his shoulders dropped a little as he relaxed. "You've got one too?" He sounded surprised.

"Yep." Ewan shrugged. "But it's not nearly as nice as this one." He offered the package again.

Dev took it, and their fingers brushed as he did so. "This one had the best reviews, not just on Amazon, but on various other sites."

Somehow it didn't surprise Ewan that Dev was the type to do his research before making a purchase. Ewan usually bought whatever was cheapest, which was how he'd ended up with his crappy, chemical-smelling, pink dildo.

"Okay, well. I guess I'd better leave you to it, then." Ewan cringed as soon as the words were out of his mouth. That sounded as though he meant he was leaving Dev and his dildo alone together—which obviously he was, but he hadn't meant it like *that*. Although now he *was* imagining what Dev might get up to with his dildo once Ewan had gone, and the thought of that sent a rush of inappropriate blood southwards. "I'm sorry again," he added lamely.

"No worries." Dev's smile was warmer and more confident now. "And I appreciate you bringing it round and explaining."

"I thought you might freak out a bit if you saw it had been opened and didn't know who by."

"You were right."

A shadow passed over Dev's features, and Ewan remembered the strength of his reaction. He wondered what had happened to Dev in the past to make him so afraid of someone knowing he liked things up his arse. "Right. Bye then."

"Bye, and thanks again."

"No worries."

Ewan closed Dev's door as he left; the snick of the lock sounded when he reached the top of the stairs.

Ewan's mind immediately went to dirty places.

Dev looked pretty innocent. Ewan wondered whether this was his first dildo, and if so, how well he'd take it. He wouldn't mind being a fly on the wall for that.

Fuck, now he had a boner. He adjusted himself as he descended the stairs. Thankfully he didn't encounter any of Dev's housemates on his way out.

Back in his own hallway, Ewan hesitated. His Pot Noodle was still waiting unopened by the kettle, but his libido won out and he headed for the stairs.

Wank first, eat later.

Then maybe wank again. He had a feeling it would take more than one jerk-off session to exorcise the mental image of Dev fucking himself with the blue dildo.

The next day, Ewan had a lie-in and then went for a run. By the time he'd showered and eaten, and then procrastinated by organising his messy desk, it was nearly two in the afternoon. Finally, he settled down to do the statistics assignment he had to finish by Monday morning.

Ewan was studying psychology. It was classed as a social science rather than science, and Ewan was more interested in the social part than the science part anyway. Maths in particular was his weak spot. Unfortunately the statistics component of the course was compulsory, and Ewan was struggling with it. He'd failed this assignment once already and his tutor had given him a second chance.

He did his best with it for a couple of hours, but was still confused by sample variance, and population variance, and googling was getting him nowhere. He thought of instant messaging a couple of people on his course, but he couldn't find anyone online.

Bored, his thoughts strayed to Dev again. Ewan had enjoyed a very satisfying session with his own dildo last night, while imagining Dev doing the same next door. The realisation that his bedroom actually shared a wall with Dev's room made the whole thing feel even dirtier, in a good way.

He thought about wanking again, but it would be nice to have some company for a change. Someone's mouth… or arse, and someone to kiss. Ewan liked foreplay but never seemed to get enough of it these days.

He sighed.

Ewan hadn't had a boyfriend since he left school. He missed it sometimes, having a person he could rely on for company and affection as well as sex. He'd made a conscious decision not to get involved with anyone in his first year. Young, free, and single seemed like a good thing to be as he enjoyed his first real taste of freedom after leaving home. But eighteen months on, he was starting to realise it wasn't all it was cracked up to be. Ewan had no trouble pulling if he went out. In a club, someone always had a ginger kink, but one-night stands — or ten-minute stands in a bathroom — were a lot less fun than they sounded. There were exceptions to every rule, of course. Ewan had had a few fun, sexy encounters, but he'd also had plenty of unsatisfying ones.

Recently he'd been using Grindr more. Chatting to someone first and flirting online was fun. Ewan had hooked up with a few guys that way. Sometimes a bit of sexting was enough to scratch the itch. You got to come with company — sort of — and sidestepped the whole awkwardness afterwards when somebody had to leave.

Ewan picked up his phone and opened the app. There were a few messages in his inbox, but none of them appealed. Scrolling through guys in his area, he did a double take when he spotted a face he recognised.

The photo was a little obscure — an artsy black-and-white shot in half-light meant Dev's face wasn't completely recognisable, but the glasses were what had caught Ewan's attention.

The description made him certain.

Virgin_geek333, 10 metres away, online now, 5' 10, 142lb. Looking for: sexual experience.

"Jesus Christ," Ewan muttered.

It must be a new profile. Ewan used Grindr a lot, and he'd never seen Dev on there before. In the photo, Dev was wearing a T-shirt that showed his collar bones, his cheeks were shaved smooth, and he looked like jailbait, even if he wasn't.

Looking for sexual experience.

The words jumped off the screen at Ewan as he stared at them, his mind whirling with horrible imaginings. Okay, Dev was probably only a year younger than Ewan, but something about him screamed innocence — and not just virginal innocence but a lack of being streetwise that would make him vulnerable to online predators. Ewan shuddered to think of the messages Dev would be getting on Grindr already. He'd be a lamb to the slaughter.

Before he could really think about what he was doing, Ewan was up and moving. He knew it was none of his business, but he didn't care.

Shoving his phone in his pocket, he ran downstairs.

CHAPTER THREE

Dev raised his head from his phone when the doorbell rang, just audible to him on the top floor. He was in the middle of an awkward conversation with someone called daddypigg_xx who kept pestering him, even though Dev had already declined his offer to "ream his sweet virgin arse."

Sure, Dev was looking for experience, but he'd been thinking more along the lines of a snog and a hand job, possibly graduating to oral eventually.

He wasn't sure of the Grindr etiquette but figured he should block this guy who obviously wasn't going to take no for an answer. But he didn't want to seem rude and make daddypigg_xx angry. Alarmingly he was only three hundred metres away, and Dev was now questioning the wisdom of putting his face on his profile.

The doorbell rang again.

Dev sighed in exasperation. It was a pain in the arse being on the top floor. Surely someone else must be in?

He opened his door and started to go downstairs, but the sound of voices told him one of his housemates had beaten him to it in the end.

"I need to talk to Dev." The voice was breathless and urgent.

Dev recognised the Scottish lilt immediately, and his heart picked up — gorgeous Ewan from next door. He flushed at the memory of their last encounter, but it had been really decent of Ewan to hand deliver the dildo and save Dev the stress of wondering who'd tampered with the parcel.

"Oh, sure. I think he's in. You know where his room is, yeah?" came Mac's reply.

"Yeah."

Dev paused on the stairs.

What the hell does Ewan want?

Not that Dev was complaining about seeing him again, but the visit was unexpected. He quickly turned and retreated to his room, but left the door ajar for Ewan. His phone's screen was flashing with another message from daddypigg_xx, so he closed the app, then ran his hands through his hair, wishing he'd put some product in it after showering earlier. It was a fluffy mess.

There was a tap on his door.

Dev looked up to see Ewan standing in the doorway. He was dressed in shorts and a T-shirt, and his feet were bare. They were nice as feet went, so pale the blue veins were clearly visible, and his nails were clean and neatly trimmed.

"I, um… came round in a hurry," Ewan said.

Dev realised he was staring at Ewan's feet, so he dragged his gaze back up to his face. "Can I help you?" Dev knew as soon as he said it that the greeting was weirdly formal. That was what happened when he spoke before thinking about what he was going to say.

Ewan just stared at him, a frown on his face and clearly uncomfortable, but Dev had no clue why. Ewan was empty-handed, so he obviously hadn't taken delivery of any more sex toys for Dev.

So what was this embarrassment about?

"This is awkward," Ewan said finally.

"Again?" Dev raised his eyebrows.

Something relaxed in Ewan's features then, and he huffed out a laugh. "Fuck… yeah. Okay, maybe this is none of my business. In fact I *know* this is none of my business, so feel free to tell me to fuck off, but I found your Grindr profile."

"Oh." Dev shrugged. "Well, I guess that's not too surprising. I mean, based on location, I suppose you would if you're on there too. I didn't see you, though."

"You wouldn't recognise me from mine," Ewan said. "My profile photo doesn't show my face."

"Right. Are you one of those blokes who only show your torso? I thought about doing that… but I think my face is a better feature. I'm a bit skinny, so I thought a torso shot would put people off. So, anyway, I still don't get it. Why are you here? If you want to hook up, you could have messaged me."

"Oh my God. No! That wasn't what I came here for."

Ouch. He obviously wasn't Ewan's type, then.

Ewan came in and shut the door behind him. He ran his hands through his hair in what looked like exasperation. They stood facing each other as Dev waited for him to explain. Dev was still confused. What on earth was Ewan's problem?

"Virgingeek. Looking for experience. Is that shit true?" Ewan finally asked.

Dev shrugged, cheeks heating as he admitted, "Yes. What's wrong with that? Everyone was a virgin once. It's nothing to be ashamed of."

"Fuck," Ewan muttered. "No, no of course it isn't. That's not what I meant… but look. Grindr's a weird place, okay? There are some nice guys who use it, and there are some not-so-nice guys, and there are some fucking dangerous weirdos. I just….

Don't you think it might be better to go on a date, find someone you trust a bit to have sex with?"

"That's what I'm trying to do." Dev was offended now. "I'm not completely naive, you know. I thought I might find someone through Grindr to hook up with, to be friends with. I'm not looking for anything serious yet, but I thought it might be a good place to start."

There was a long pause.

"Well. Okay. What about me, then?" Ewan blurted.

Dev blinked. "What about you?"

"I mean... I could help you with that. Getting experience. I might not be your type or whatever, but I could show you the ropes as it were—I don't mean in a kinky way... unless you're into being tied up. And you already know me, so you know I'm not an axe murderer or anything."

"I don't know you well. You *could* be an axe murderer."

"Yeah. But I'm not."

"I think that's what any axe murderer would say." Dev was utterly serious. It was logical after all, but Ewan laughed.

"Yeah. I guess so. Bloody hell, Dev. You're hard to argue with. But seriously, though. The offer's there. You want sexual experience?" He gestured to himself in a way that drew Dev's gaze to the tempting bulge in the stretchy fabric of his shorts. "I'm here for you. No strings, no pressure. I'm not looking for a relationship. But if you want someone to have some fun with, then I'm up for it."

He seemed to be serious. Dev considered his options. Ewan was a nice guy from what Dev had seen so far. He absolutely *was* Dev's type, and the sexy accent was a bonus. Ewan lived next door, so he had geography on his side when it came to convenience. Dev had no way of checking his credentials, but he wouldn't have been able to ask for sexual references for anonymous guys on Grindr either. It was a good offer. Dev would be churlish to turn Ewan down. But he didn't want to inconvenience him or abuse his obviously generous nature, as Ewan was clearly only doing this to be kind. But hell, even if it was only a pity fuck, Dev would take it over daddypigg reaming his arse any day of the week.

"That's really kind of you," he said. "But I don't want to take advantage. Is there something I could do for you in return?"

Ewan made an odd noise, somewhere between a cough and a choke. "Um…." He scanned Dev's room until his eyes lit on the rows of textbooks. "You're a physics student?"

Dev nodded.

"So you must be pretty good at maths, right?"

Dev nodded again. It seemed like bragging to mention that he'd won the maths prize at school. His maths teacher had been devastated when he'd applied to study physics instead of mathematics at university. But physics was even more exciting than maths, especially cosmology.

"Well, I study psychology, and I have to do statistics as part of my course. But I really suck at it. Seriously, numbers are a mystery to me. So could you help me with that? And in return I'll help you with… the other stuff."

Dev smiled, happy their arrangement could be a reciprocal one. "Yes, that's a good idea." Then he frowned as another thought occurred to him. "Do you think we ought to put something in writing? Like a contract?"

Ewan's lips twitched, but his face remained serious. "I don't see the need for that."

"Okay." Dev stuck out his hand. "Let's shake on it. A gentleman's agreement, if you will."

Ewan's hand was warm and strong, and the touch of his lightly calloused palm made Dev imagine how it would feel on other parts of his body. The thought that he would be finding out exactly how that felt very soon was enough to make him flush all the way to the tips of his ears.

Ewan grinned at him. "When do you want to start?"

Dev cleared his throat. "Well… I need time to make a list of exactly what I want to learn from you."

"Of course you do."

The amusement in Ewan's tone made Dev look at him sharply. Was he taking the piss? Dev wasn't always good at knowing when he was being teased, which was part of what made him an easy target for bullies.

But Ewan added, "It's fine. It would be useful to know what you want to do, and if there's anything you don't want to do."

"Okay, I'll do that soon. I guess maybe we could start next weekend? No point in delaying, but we're probably both quite busy during the week."

"Yeah. Actually…."

Ewan rubbed his chin, drawing Dev's attention to the pale orange stubble that covered his jaw. The freckles that sprinkled his nose were almost the same pale golden brown as his eyes. "I have a stats assignment due on Monday, and I'm really struggling with it. I don't suppose you could help me out with that tomorrow, could you?"

"Okay, sure." Dev felt a thrill of excitement at getting started. Maybe working on statistics would be less fun than learning about sex, but he liked numbers, and the idea of getting to spend some time with Ewan was appealing. If he got to know him better, then it might feel more natural to have sex with him. Because although he liked the idea of that—he *really* liked the idea of that—it was also pretty terrifying at the same time.

What if Dev was awful at it? Just because he was a good student at academic subjects didn't mean he'd be any good at kissing, or blow jobs, or any of the other things he'd seen people doing to each other on the Internet.

"Shall I bring my work over here? Or do you want to come to mine?" Ewan asked.

"I'll come to yours," Dev said. "And I'll bring my list over then, too, so that we can talk about where to start next weekend."

"What—?" Ewan frowned. "Oh, *that* list." His cheeks turned pink, making his freckles less visible for a moment. "Yes, okay."

"What time?" Dev picked up his phone and opened his calendar.

"Um... twoish?"

"Do you mean two's okay? Or would you rather I came a bit later?" Dev liked to be clear about those things.

Ewan's lips curved for a moment before he replied. "Two's fine."

Dev typed it into his phone for two o'clock: *Help Ewan with stats*. "Okay." He smiled. "I'll see you then."

"Right. And Dev... maybe you should consider editing your Grindr profile for now? Tone it down a little so you sound less... I dunno, or make your profile more anonymous, perhaps?"

"Yeah, maybe you're right."

"Okay. See you tomorrow."

And with that, Ewan turned and went.

Dev took a deep breath and let it out slowly. Well... it seemed as if Grindr had helped him find what he was looking for, after all. If only indirectly. He opened his phone again, pulled up the app, and winced when he saw a message from someone called holedestroyer1965. Dev promptly deleted his profile without reading the message. He could always make another one when he was sexually experienced and ready to roll.

CHAPTER FOUR

Ewan was lugging the vacuum cleaner up the stairs when he met Nadia coming in the other direction.

"Bloody hell, that's a first," Nadia said as she retreated back to the landing to let him past.

"Thanks," he panted as he reached the top and set his burden down. "And fuck off. I hoover my room sometimes."

She arched a dark eyebrow. "Yeah, like the time you dropped a bag of Doritos on the floor when you were pissed and then walked all over them in the night."

"Well, yes. Like that time." He glared at her. Nadia's memory was far too good.

"Better once—sorry, twice—than never, I guess." She grinned and Ewan softened. It was hard to be annoyed with Nadia for long. "So, what's the occasion? Hot date?"

Ewan hesitated a fraction too long before answering. "No, I'm just helping a friend with an assignment."

"A friend." She didn't look convinced. "You don't usually clean for friends."

"Well, you know. The muck on my floor has reached critical mass, so…."

"Okay, then. Have fun, with your *friend*." She passed him and started to go down the stairs.

Ewan wasn't sure how much fun an afternoon of statistics would be, but it would be better with Dev's company than struggling through it alone. "Thanks," he said to her retreating back. "I will."

By the time two o'clock came around, Ewan's room was almost unrecognisable. It wasn't up to Dev's standards of clean and tidy, but it wasn't Ewan's usual bomb site, by any means. Admittedly he'd hidden a lot of dirty clothes and other crap under his bed, but on the surface it looked pretty good. The bed was made—not with clean sheets, that was a step too far, but the covers were straight and he had cleared enough space on his desk for two people to work at it. And most amazingly of all, he could actually see the bits of carpet that weren't covered by furniture.

Ewan stood back and surveyed his handiwork. It looked pretty nice like that. Maybe he should try a little harder to keep it tidy even when he wasn't trying to impress someone.

He wasn't entirely sure why he'd made so much effort, but Dev seemed so fastidious and organised. Ewan didn't want him to find out he was a hot mess and be turned off before they'd even got started with anything sexual.

God. His heart thumped harder as he imagined how that might go. He wasn't entirely sure what had happened yesterday and honestly hadn't intended on offering his services as a sexpert when he rushed around to Dev's house. He hadn't really been thinking much at all, beyond wanting to warn Dev that his Grindr profile would be like catnip to the creepiest predators on the internet, and suggesting that maybe he should tone down all the "virgin seeks experience" stuff a little. Then he'd opened his mouth and said things without thinking — that happened to him a lot — and he'd promised.

A gentleman's agreement, as Dev had called it.

The things Ewan was imagining doing to Dev weren't very gentlemanly, but better Ewan than some creep on Grindr. Whatever happened, he was going to make sure Dev enjoyed himself. Ewan's first times for everything had been with someone he liked, someone he trusted. He wanted to be that person for Dev.

The sound of the doorbell had him running down the stairs. It was two on the dot, so he reckoned it must be Dev. Already, Ewan had the feeling Dev was the sort of person to be utterly punctual.

Ryan beat him to the front door. When Ewan got there, he could just see Dev's face over Ryan's shoulder.

"Yeah?" Ryan said.

"I'm here to see Ewan," Dev said, raising his chin as though he'd been challenged. "To help him with his statistics."

"Hi, Dev," Ewan called. "Let him in, Ry."

Ryan stepped aside so Dev could slip past him.

"Cheers," Ewan said to Ryan. Then to Dev, "Shall we go up? Or do you want a drink or anything?"

"No thanks."

"Okay, then, I'm up the top like you." Ewan led the way, keenly aware of Dev following and suddenly very conscious of his arse and what Dev might think of it. Ewan had a good arse, in his own opinion. Hopefully Dev would agree.

He let Dev into his room and closed the door behind them. It was a decent-sized room for a student house, but with Dev in it, Ewan was suddenly almost claustrophobic, as if there wasn't enough air for both of them. His heart was racing and his hands prickled with sweat.

He's here to help you with your maths, for fuck's sake, he reminded himself. *Chill!*

"So, um... have a seat." He gestured vaguely at the desk. He'd borrowed a chair from downstairs so there would be one for each of them.

"Thanks." Dev sat on the wooden chair from downstairs, leaving the comfier desk chair for Ewan.

Ewan sat beside him and spread out his papers. "So this is what I'm working on. I've made a start, but I'm not sure if what I've done already is right. Maybe you should start by checking it."

"Sure — oh, hang on." Dev shifted in his seat, reached into his back pocket, and pulled out a neatly folded page from a notebook. "Let me give you this now so I don't forget. It's my list."

Dev held it out to Ewan, his hand shaking slightly. Maybe he was feeling as nervous and awkward as Ewan.

Ewan stared into Dev's dark brown eyes. With long, thick lashes, they were ridiculously beautiful. Dev licked his lips, drawing Ewan's attention to those instead. That didn't help matters; his mouth was pretty too.

"It's my list of things I want to learn about," Dev said. "Sex things."

Ewan swallowed. "Yeah. I got that."

He took the piece of paper. Looking at it now was probably a bad idea. He was supposed to be thinking about numbers... but instead he was thinking about Dev's pink lips around his cock. Surely oral had to be on the list?

Please let it be on the list.

"Can I look now?" His voice was a dry scrape. He cleared his throat. "I mean… it's probably better to check it while you're here, in case there's anything that I—I mean anything that's…."

He had no idea what the fuck he meant.

"In case there's anything too kinky on there?" Dev's brow furrowed. "I hope not. But you don't have to do anything you don't want to."

Ewan let out a breathless chuckle, because that should be *his* line. Who was the virgin here, anyway? "Yeah, of course."

"Go on, then." Dev nodded to the list.

Ewan unfolded it carefully. The paper stuck to his sweaty fingers.

Dev's handwriting was small, slightly spiky, and perfectly formed. Much like him. The title was underlined and the items were bullet-pointed. Ewan was surprised there weren't checkboxes so they could tick things off as they went.

As Ewan read down the list. His cheeks got hot and his dick got hard.

<u>Sex Things to Try</u>
Kissing
Hand jobs
Frottage
Blow jobs (giving)
Blow jobs (receiving)
Fingering
Rimming (giving)
Rimming (receiving)
Topping

Bottoming

"So?"

Dev's voice brought Ewan back from a detailed fantasy where he was doing all those things with Dev in a mental slideshow of bare flesh, jizz, and lube. He blinked several times as he became aware of his surroundings again.

Dev's cheeks were flushed but his expression was serious. "I think I've got all the basics there, but if there's anything on the list you're not into, that's fine."

"No, no… this is all okay with me."

It was more than okay. Ewan hadn't actually tried rimming—either way around—before. His ex hadn't been into the idea of it, and doing it with some random person from a hook-up app hadn't appealed. He thought about mentioning his lack of experience in that area to Dev but decided against it. He was sure he could wing it, and he didn't want Dev to lose confidence in his abilities. "But how do you know if it's going to be okay with you? I mean… if you haven't done any of this stuff before?"

Dev shrugged. "I want to try it—then I'll know what I like. At the moment I don't even know if I'm a top, a bottom, or vers—or none of the above. Not all gay guys even like anal, but I won't know until I try."

His logic was flawless. Ewan shifted in his seat, hoping his gigantic boner wasn't too obvious. He glanced down at Dev's lap, but the creasing of his rather baggy jeans gave nothing away. "Okay, then," Ewan said lamely. "It all looks good to me."

Dev cleared his throat. "Now, about safety. I think we should both get tested. I'm a virgin, so it's highly unlikely I'd test positive for any STDs, but I don't think it's fair of me to expect you to take my word for it. So I suggest we both make an appointment to get tested this week. And then I'd like us to be exclusive as long as this arrangement continues. Would that be okay with you?"

"Um, yeah. But, I—" Ewan was scrambling to keep up with Dev's rapid-fire speech. He was adorably intense when he talked like this. The little furrow in his brow and the way he moved his hands made it hard to focus on the words.

"Not that I want to bareback...," Dev went on. "That would still be too risky without waiting for three months and testing again, but for oral I did some research, and the risk of HIV transmission is pretty low. So if we both test negative for everything, then I'd like to have unprotected oral if that's okay with you, so long as you're happy to be monogamous while we're working through the list?"

"Sure." Ewan didn't trust himself to say anything else at that point. Dev had it all figured out. Ewan got tested regularly, anyway. He was sensible like that, but if he was starting something new with Dev, it was only fair for Dev to see the proof that it was safe.

"So, I could make appointments for both of us if you like?"

Ewan nodded.

Dev got out his phone and entered something into his reminders. "Can I take your number? Then I'll text you the date and time. They do evening appointments. Is there any day you can't do?"

"No." Ewan reeled off his number, and Dev added that to his phone too.

"Okay, then." Dev put his phone back in his pocket and adjusted his glasses. He pulled Ewan's work across the desk so he could see it properly. "Let's take a look at this assignment."

His brain still catching up with the gear change, Ewan tried to get his mind away from rimming and back to statistics.

The next two hours passed in an agony of sexual tension—for Ewan, at least. Dev seemed remarkably composed as he picked through Ewan's work, finding and correcting errors and explaining what Ewan had done wrong. He was a good teacher. Despite obviously being light years ahead of Ewan in mathematical ability, Dev had the surprising knack of being able to explain things in a way that made sense.

Ewan's concentration wasn't the best. Dev's proximity, the brush of their elbows, the way he tapped his slim fingers on the desk when he was concentrating, and the just-perceptible scent of his skin and hair drove Ewan crazy. All of those things tugged at the edges of his consciousness to drag his mind away from facts and figures and back to a persistent fantasy of throwing Dev down on the desk and sucking his considerable brains out through his dick.

Finally, when Dev had fixed Ewan's mistakes and made sure he understood what he still needed to do in order to finish, Dev leaned back in his chair. "So, are you okay now? You should have everything you need to get this done tonight."

Ewan put his pen down and sighed. He was tired, but way less stressed about the assignment now. "Yeah. Thank you so much."

"If you get stuck again, you know where I am."

"I think I'll be fine. You're an awesome teacher."

Dev gave a small shy smile. "Thanks. I often used to help friends at school, so I'm used to doing it."

"Dumbing things down for us lesser mortals?" Ewan grinned.

Dev's smile widened. "Yeah, well. You'll be returning the favour soon enough."

Just like that, the electric tension was back. They stared at each other, and Ewan could feel each thud of his heart.

"Okay, I'm going to go." Dev broke eye contact and pushed his chair back so he could stand. "I'll text you about the appointments."

"Right." Ewan's gaze fell to the list, still open on his desk, where he'd pushed it aside while they worked. "Um, hang on." He stood up too and moved so they were facing each other. "Do you think, maybe we should check… I mean. What if there's no chemistry between us? Do we really want to get tested and then wait till next weekend to find out if this is going to work? Wouldn't it be better to be sure?"

"Maybe." The corners of Dev's mouth tugged down. "But—"

"I'm sure it will be fine," Ewan rushed to reassure him. "But I thought perhaps…." He swallowed. "We could try the first thing on the list now, just to see. There's no need to be tested for kissing. We can't catch anything that way."

Dev frowned. "Well… unless one of us has a cold. But I feel pretty healthy, and you seem okay too. There's glandular fever, of course. That can be transmitted by kissing, but I had that when I was fifteen, and it's rare to get it twice—"

Ewan put a finger on Dev's lips. "Stop talking, Dev. I want to kiss you. Can I?"

Dev froze, dark eyes wide, lips softly parted against Ewan's fingertip. He nodded, a tiny jerk of his head.

"Have you ever kissed anyone before?" Ewan asked.

That time Dev's head moved from side to side. A definite no.

"Not even a girl?"

Dev shook again.

"How is that possible?" Ewan couldn't imagine his teenage years without messy, fumbling kisses. With girls, and then eventually with boys—or one boy in particular. But teen years were all about snogging, and boasting about snogging, and pretending you'd snogged someone even if you hadn't.

Dev opened his mouth to answer, but knowing Dev, the explanation would be overly detailed, and Ewan had meant it as a rhetorical question anyway. Ewan was done talking. "Never mind." He moved his hand to cup Dev's jaw.

Dev's lips stayed parted, and he swallowed, his Adam's apple bobbing in his slender neck. The faintest trace of stubble rasped Ewan's palm, a sexy reminder of Dev's masculinity despite his doe eyes and soft lips that a supermodel—male or female—would envy.

Ewan was a couple of inches taller, so he had to tilt his head down to reach Dev's lips. He brushed them lightly with his own, pressing soft, closed-mouth kisses there until Dev brought his hands up and settled them on Ewan's waist, moving closer, giving himself up to the kiss.

They parted their lips and tried to deepen it, noses bumping when they both tilted the same way. Ewan used both hands on Dev's face now, guiding him. As first kisses went it was predictably far from perfect. Not enough tongue at first, and then a little too much as Dev got overeager. But there was a sweet intensity to it, too, that surged through Ewan from his scalp to his toes.

Dev made a small broken sound, pulling Ewan closer by his hips, and Dev was as hard as Ewan was, and suddenly nothing else in the world mattered other than where their bodies connected: lips melding, hands clutching each other, cocks pressed together.

Dev finally pulled away, suddenly, as though in shock. He wiped his mouth with the back of his hand and stared at Ewan, breathing hard. "I... uh.... I should go."

"Yeah." Ewan blinked, a little dazed. It was probably for the best if they stopped, unless Dev wanted to tick off more things on his list today.

"As for the question of chemistry...." Dev let his gaze drop to the bulge in Ewan's sweatpants, which hid nothing. Dev reached down and adjusted his own dick. "I don't think that's going to be a problem."

Ewan grinned. "Nope. You gonna go and jerk off now?"

Dev's face flamed, but he grinned back. "Yes."

"Me too."

"God. Okay, I'm really going now."

"I would see you out, but—" Ewan gestured to his cock, which was trying to drill through the fabric.

"Yeah. No worries. Okay, bye Ewan. See you soon."

"Bye, Dev."

As soon as the door shut behind Dev, Ewan had his hand in his pants stroking his dick. He threw himself down on his bed, arching up into his fist. It only took a few minutes before he was groaning and coming all over his hand and stomach as he imagined Dev on the other side of the wall doing the exact same thing.

"Holy shit," Ewan muttered weakly when his brain started to function again.

Next weekend couldn't come fast enough.

CHAPTER FIVE

Dev phoned Student Health Services on Monday afternoon to make appointments for himself and Ewan.

"It's for me and… a friend," he explained.

"That's fine," the woman on the end of the phone said cheerfully. "We can see you one after the other if you come in at 4:30 on Wednesday. Can I take your names?"

Awkward. Dev didn't know Ewan's surname. "Mine's Devrim Karadere." He spelled it out for her. "And he's called Ewan. Um… I don't actually know his second name."

The confession didn't seem to faze her. "No problem. So we'll see you and Ewan on Wednesday at four thirty, then. Okay?"

"Okay, bye."

Dev ended the call, his heart beating fast. He didn't like making phone calls at the best of times, and that had been a particularly nerve-racking one. Necessary, though. He was determined to do it right.

Next he texted Ewan.

We have appointments at Student Health on Weds at 4.30 for STI testing. Is that time okay for you?

He pressed Send before he remembered Ewan didn't have his contact details yet. So he sent another message. *This is Dev, by the way, in case that wasn't obvious.*

Ewan didn't reply for a while, and Dev started to get nervous. Maybe he was having second thoughts? Dev was trying to study, but he was unusually distracted, his normal ability to hyperfocus shattered by memories of kissing Ewan yesterday. It had been the best thing Dev ever felt, a perfect blend of nerves and excitement that exploded into bliss when he gave himself up to the sensations of Ewan's lips and the scratch of his stubble. When he got back to his room afterwards, he wanked twice just thinking about it. The first time had been a biological necessity, but the second time, Dev had indulged himself in a wonderful blend of recollection and fantasy.

If it felt so good to kiss Ewan, what on earth would it be like when they took things further?

The chime of his phone made Dev jump. He was hard and his hand was on the bulge in his jeans. He snatched it away to read the message.

I worked out it was you by a process of elimination. You're the only dude I've arranged to go on an STI testing date with this week ;) And yes half four on Weds is fine.

Dev was relieved the wink emoticon was there to make the tone clear. The word *date* gave him a little thrill, even though Ewan was joking.

Good, he replied, knowing it was a pathetically weak attempt to keep the conversation going.

Text conversations weren't Dev's strong point. Socially awkward at the best of times, at least face-to-face he had more to go on if he remembered to pay attention to the visual cues. But he couldn't turn up on Ewan's doorstep to talk. They didn't have that kind of friendship... not yet. So it had to be text or nothing.

Ewan texted back.

I have a lecture on campus that finishes at 4, so I'll meet you there.

Okay, Dev typed. Then feeling brave, he added more.

Maybe we could go for a coffee or something afterwards?

Dev didn't actually drink coffee — he thought it was bitter and gross — but meeting someone for coffee was one of those things people didn't mean literally.

Ewan's reply was almost immediate. *That sounds great :)*

Dev frowned at his phone, trying to work out whether it felt like the end of the conversation or not. There wasn't a question, so maybe it would be too pushy to text back again.

God, never mind learning about sex acts, he needed a rulebook for social interaction. He'd looked up plenty of those online as a younger teenager, when he'd realised that stuff didn't come naturally to him. He managed fine most of the time these days, and the Internet was a good source of self-help.

He was about to let it go and put his phone down, when another message flashed up.

Yesterday was fun. And then before Dev could think of what to reply again, Ewan added, *I meant the kissing part rather than the statistics part, in case *that* wasn't obvious ;)*

Dev laughed, happiness fizzing in his belly like sweet lemonade.

Yes, the kissing part was — he wanted to type something effusive: amazing, life-changing, multiple-orgasm-inducing, but he settled on *pretty great.*

The understatement of the century.

His phone remained silent after that, and although part of him was disappointed they hadn't continued the conversation, he was still ridiculously happy for the rest of the evening.

On Wednesday, Dev was in a state of nervous anticipation that had him missing things in lectures and staring into space as the day progressed. His last class finished at two, so he went home for a late lunch before going up to his room to get changed.

It wasn't a date, not really, but Ewan had used the word date, and they were going for generic coffee after their appointment. That certainly sounded date-like, if you left the whole STI-testing thing aside. Whatever it was, Dev wanted to make the effort to look presentable.

When he was younger, Dev had zero interest in fashion. When other boys at school cared about what brand their trainers and jeans were, Dev only minded whether they were comfortable. If it was socially acceptable, Dev would still wear pyjamas or sweatpants all day with the softest, baggiest T-shirts he could find.

When he was a little kid, that was exactly what he'd done. His mum had always cut out the scratchy labels and bought him things with elasticated waistbands. However, when puberty struck and other kids started to care what they looked like, Dev quickly realised he was going to need to fall in line unless he wanted to be teased more than he already was. At least at school there was a uniform, so he didn't stand out. But at the weekends when he went out, he learned to wear uncomfortable jeans with time-wasting zips and buttons, and he chose trainers that looked like the ones his friends wore and T-shirts from shops that were 'cool.' Dev didn't get it. Why was a T-shirt from Superdry better than an almost-identical one from Asda, just because it cost three times as much? But Dev wanted to fit in as much as he could, so he went along with it.

He kept on his usual jeans. They were his favourites, a little too baggy to be properly cool, but he had his limits. He decided to change his shirt, though. The one he'd been wearing was boring black. He liked it because it was well-washed and comfortable, but it didn't do much for his appearance. So he took it off and pulled on a grey T-shirt instead.

Dev looked critically in the mirror. The T-shirt was a little snugger than the ones he usually wore. Naturally lean, Dev had never seen the inside of a gym. He kept fit by walking everywhere, and didn't have an ounce of fat on him. There wasn't a lot of muscle either, and he frowned. What was Ewan's normal type? Maybe he preferred bigger, broader guys like himself. Ewan wasn't bulky, but he had a much more athletic build than Dev. He looked fit and strong.

Dev sighed, self-conscious about his bony elbows and skinny arms. He went to his wardrobe and dug out a checked shirt in shades of dark blue and green. He put it on over his T-shirt and did up a few of the buttons, then rolled up the sleeves to mid-forearm. That was better. He felt safer, less on display.

The thought occurred to him that he'd be getting naked with Ewan eventually, and that was both thrilling and frightening. At least Ewan was a nice guy. Even if Dev's skinny body didn't push Ewan's buttons, Dev was sure he wouldn't be mean about it.

Dev got to Student Health ten minutes early. He booked in at reception, trying to sound completely normal and confident, as though having an STI check was something he did every day. His face burned, but he managed to say his name and the time of his appointment without sounding too strangled.

"Okay, Devrim. Take a seat in the waiting area. They're running on time today, so you won't have to wait long."

Dev sat and immediately got out his phone. Thank God for smartphones. What on earth had people done in the days before they existed? All the waiting rooms he'd ever been in still had a pile of dog-eared magazines on a table somewhere, but most people ignored them.

He checked his emails and found one from his mum with a link to a cookery website.

Maybe you could try some of these recipes, the message read. *You can search their database by level of difficulty and how long they take to cook. I don't like to think of you eating processed rubbish.*

Dev wasn't enjoying the processed rubbish either, so he made a note in his reminders to check out the site later.

Just then, the sound of the door to the waiting area made him look up. Relief flooded him when he saw Ewan. Not that he'd thought Ewan wouldn't show, but Dev was glad he was on time. The smile on Ewan's face made Dev's stomach flop alarmingly. Was it normal to feel like that when you saw someone for the first time after kissing them?

"Hi." Ewan stopped in front of him, smiling.

"Hi." Dev stared back.

Dressed in a burgundy hoodie that contrasted beautifully with his bright red hair, and slim-cut jeans that hugged his muscular thighs and the soft bulge at his crotch, Ewan looked good enough to eat—literally. Dev's mouth watered as he imagined what was under Ewan's clothes. He hoped the test results would be fast; he was totally ready to get onto the oral sex items on his list.

"Hello, do you have an appointment?"

The receptionist's chirpy voice interrupted their meaningful silence.

"Oh, um, yeah." Ewan turned away and went to the desk. "I'm Ewan Campbell, I have an appointment."

"Campbell…." She typed something and then frowned, scrolling on her computer. "I can't find you on the list."

"I made the appointment for both of us." Dev got up quickly and went over to the desk again. "I only gave his first name." He glanced sideways at Ewan and flushed.

"Oh right, yes." She studied her screen again. "There you are. Sorry about that."

"No worries," Ewan said.

Neither he nor the receptionist seemed ruffled by the awkwardness.

Ewan and Dev went back to the chairs, and Ewan sat down next to Dev.

"Sorry," Dev muttered, still embarrassed. "I forgot to ask for your surname."

"Well, you know it now. I'm Ewan Campbell. It's nice to meet you." He grinned and held out a hand.

Dev chuckled. "Devrim Karadere, and likewise." He took Ewan's hand and shook.

Their eyes met, and Dev lost himself in the depths of Ewan's. They were gorgeous. No one colour could describe them. Dark brown at the edges bled into something richer and warmer, leading to a glow of liquid gold around his pupils. Pupils that were large as they stared at each other, hands still clasped together.

Dev finally broke away, warned off by the heat in his groin and the tingle in his balls.

Not here. Not now.

"So, you're Scottish?"

"Yeah." Ewan settled back into the chair beside him and stretched his legs out. "The name would give it away even if the accent didn't, huh? I'm from Edinburgh. My mum always jokes that I couldn't have moved farther away for uni if I'd tried, but it wasn't personal. I just liked the sound of Plymouth, and I wanted to learn to surf."

"Have you?"

"Not yet. But it's on my list of things to get around to."

"You have a list?" Dev perked up. Lists were familiar ground.

"Well… only a list in my head. You know how it is."

Dev didn't know. His lists were always on paper, or on his phone, or on his computer. But he nodded anyway. "Yeah."

"So, Devrim Kara…?"

"Karadere. I'm half–Turkish Cypriot. My father came here with his family in the seventies."

A door that led off the waiting room opened, and a woman in a nurse's uniform came out. She looked at them both and smiled. "Devrim and Ewan. Who wants to go first?"

Dev looked at Ewan, who shrugged.

"I will, then," Dev said.

"Okay, come on in."

The appointment was very straightforward. She asked Dev lots of questions about his sexual history and didn't bat an eyelid when he answered no to everything.

"I want the test results so I can show Ewan," he explained. "He shouldn't have to take my word for it. We don't know each other very well—yet."

"That's very sensible of you," she said. "I wish all the young people I see had that kind of attitude."

After she'd taken a blood sample, she gave Dev a little pot with a screw-top lid. "Just pop to the toilets here to do me a urine sample if you can, and leave it with Reception. If you can't manage one now, you can drop it in tomorrow. We have to send the samples away for testing, but we should have the results back by Wednesday next week, so you can drop by to collect them after that." She smiled. "Right, send your boyfriend in next."

"Um… he's not—" Dev cut himself off quickly, realising he was in danger of sharing too much. "Okay, thanks."

He left the door ajar on his way out. "You're up," he said to Ewan. "I have to go pee in a jar. I'll wait for you out here afterwards."

Dev struggled at first—his bladder didn't want to cooperate. Sitting on the toilet seat in the single cubicle, he had to imagine waterfalls and showers before it finally flowed. But eventually he managed to fill up the little jar.

When Dev emerged, Ewan was on his way into the toilets, a jar in his hand too.

"Success?" He grinned.

"Yeah." Dev hid the bottle in his hand. Ewan didn't need to see his urine — unless he was into that, and Dev sincerely hoped he wasn't.

"Wish me luck." Ewan brushed past him on his way to the cubicle.

CHAPTER SIX

As he stepped out of the health centre into watery April sunshine, Ewan held the door open for Dev, who gave him a shy smile.

They stopped on the pavement outside. It had rained earlier, and the ground was still damp underfoot. Now the sky was pale blue between patches of grey and white cloud. Seagulls screamed overhead, their shrill voices carried on the breeze.

"So, where do you want to go?" Ewan was looking forward to spending some time with Dev and getting to know him better.

"The Student Union café?" The breeze lifted Dev's dark hair, ruffling it, and he brushed his fringe out of his eyes.

"Okay."

It was only about a five-minute walk away and was one of the cheapest places around. As they walked, Ewan asked, "So, do you want to start your, er, lessons with me this weekend?" He tried to sound casual.

Dev shrugged. "Don't you think we should wait for the test results? I could help you with your maths again, though."

Ewan thought he'd die of sexual frustration if he had to sit through another tutoring session with Dev, with no promise of more at the end of it. "You don't need test results for hand jobs. We could start with that." He glanced sidelong at Dev, who kept his gaze fixed on the path in front of him. "And more kissing, of course—if you want?"

Dev snapped his head up then and met Ewan's gaze as though checking his expression for something. Ewan wasn't sure what Dev was looking for.

"Yes," Dev said emphatically. "Yes. I, um, I think I need more practice at that." He looked ahead again, but a smile tugged at the corners of his lips.

"You did very well for a beginner," Ewan said.

Another shy glance sideways from Dev, and Ewan grinned.

Dev smiled back. "Thanks." His cheeks went pink. "So, yeah. This weekend sounds good. When are you free?"

"I don't have any plans. How about Friday night?" Not that Ewan was impatient or anything.

"Sure. Maths and then hand jobs?" Dev's voice was completely serious, but Ewan couldn't keep a straight face.

He chuckled. "Yeah, I guess. It would be a bit of a downer to go from sex to maths. The sex can be the reward after all that studying."

"But for me the sex *is* the studying. So what do I get as a reward?"

"Hmm. That's tricky. Well, I guess if you get me off first, then your reward is getting to come afterwards." Heat prickled down Ewan's spine at that thought and his cock thickened.

"Sounds fair." Dev's voice was a little strangled.

Movement in Ewan's peripheral vision made him look and catch Dev adjusting himself. Ewan was glad he wasn't the only one affected by the conversation — some intense verbal foreplay, and they had another two days before they got to follow through. But knowing he had to wait somehow made it all the more exciting.

They'd reached the Student Union, and they made their way to the café. It was fairly busy, but there were some tables free, so they went to bag one.

"Do you know what you want?" Ewan asked. "I'm not sure what I fancy yet, but I can go and order for both of us if you already know?"

"Yeah. I'll have chocolate milkshake, please." Dev pulled out a chair and sat down.

"Anything to eat?"

"No thanks. But can you get me the deluxe one with the whipped cream? Then it's kind of like a meal anyway."

"Sure."

Ewan went up to order, trying to decide what he was in the mood for. He ended up buying a cup of tea and a danish pastry.

Ewan carried the laden tray back to their table and sat down. "Here you go." He passed Dev his milkshake.

"Thanks." Dev pushed some coins across the table towards him.

"Oh, you didn't need to…."

But Dev shrugged and didn't take the money back, so Ewan pocketed it, feeling a little… not hurt, exactly, but put in his place, maybe? He reminded himself it wasn't a date. There probably wasn't a name for what it was—not hanging out with a friend either, because he didn't know Dev that well yet. Whatever else happened between them, Ewan hoped Dev would eventually become a friend, because he was drawn to him in a way that was hard to quantify. Dev was cute, sure, but

Ewan's fascination was born of more than just his physical appeal. Dev was a peculiar mixture of shy and forward, and Ewan never knew what to expect from him. It was unsettling but exciting too.

"So." Ewan aimed to keep the conversation away from anything that would give him a hard-on. "Tell me more about your family. What are they like? What do your parents do? Where's home for you? Wow, that's a lot of questions, sorry." He smiled.

Dev smiled too. "That's okay. I like questions. It means I know what to say, so there's no awkward silences."

If it was anyone else, Ewan would think he was joking, but with Dev, he knew it was the truth.

"So." Dev ticked his replies off on his fingers as he answered. "My family are… I don't know, pretty great, I guess? I get on well with my parents most of the time. I have a sister—she's six years older, so she doesn't live at home anymore. My dad's a doctor, and my mum works for a charity. They live in Oxford."

"Do they know you're gay?" Ewan asked.

"Yes." Dev scooped some of the cream off the top of his milkshake with a straw. "I told them when I was seventeen, but I think they'd guessed ages before. I'd never been interested in girls, and I'd plastered my bedroom wall with burly superheroes and sometimes footballers or rugby players, even though I hate sports. That was a bit of a giveaway, I think." He popped the cream in his mouth, his dark eyes fixed on Ewan as his lips closed around the straw.

"I guess it would be. And are they okay with it?"

"Yeah, they are. But my dad's brother is gay, so he kind of forged the way for me. I think things were tough for him when he came out. My grandparents weren't at all understanding. He hid it for a long time." Dev had a faraway look and his mouth turned down. "I feel lucky I didn't have to do that. So, how about you? Tell me about your family. Same questions."

"Okay, well," Ewan tried to remember what he'd asked Dev. "I'm from Edinburgh. My dad works in finance and my mum's a nurse. I've got a younger brother and a younger sister, both still at school. My family's okay. I wouldn't say we were close, but we're not super dysfunctional either. Both my parents work too hard, so they're grumpy and stressed a lot of the time. It's kind of a relief to be away from that, but I miss them too."

"And do they know you're gay?"

"Yeah. I came out when I had a boyfriend at school. We both wanted to tell our families. It was a shock to my parents. They really didn't see it coming, and although they're okay with it—like they say all the right things and are supportive and all—" Ewan paused trying to find the right words to describe how he felt around his parents. "—I dunno. Something's changed. They look at me differently now, as if I'm not the same person I was before? Maybe it's just me being paranoid, but that's how I feel." Ewan stopped, embarrassed at spilling his guts to Dev like that. He fiddled with a teaspoon, staring at his warped reflection in the metal, unwilling to meet Dev's gaze and show his vulnerability.

Dev reached across the table and took the teaspoon out of Ewan's hand, then tangled their fingers together and squeezed. The sympathetic touch eased the ache in Ewan's chest. He let his gaze slide up to meet Dev's and saw understanding there. He gave Dev a tentative smile.

"Well, look who it is!" A loud, mocking voice from behind Ewan made Dev start and drop Ewan's hand as though it were on fire.

Ewan turned to see a group of three blokes, all with matching mocking grins on their faces as they looked at him and Dev.

"Hey, Dev*reem*." The same voice as before, belonging to a skinny guy with brown hair, a scruffy half-arsed attempt at a beard, and mean eyes. "You finally found someone with a real dick to fuck, then? Look out, mate," he addressed Ewan. "This one's into some weird shit."

Ewan pushed his chair back with a screech and squared up to him. "What's your fucking problem?"

Beardy Guy's attitude shifted immediately to unease. Ewan was taller, bigger, and angrier than he was, and he suddenly looked as though he realised he was picking on the wrong guy. "I… uh…."

Ewan continued in a menacing tone. "I don't know who you are, and I don't give a shit because you're not worth my time. But you and your friends are interrupting us, so why don't you fuck off before I break your nose."

Ewan had barely been in a fight in his life, but he'd played rugby at school and was pretty sure he could handle this twat. Beardy Guy's two sidekicks were already backing off, so it didn't look like he was going to get much support from them.

"It's okay, Ewan. Just drop it." Dev was standing behind him now, and he put a hand on the tense muscles of Ewan's shoulder.

Ewan looked around and realised that all eyes in the café were on the unfolding drama.

"Yeah, you should piss off like he says," called a girl from a couple of tables over, glaring at Beardy Guy. "Take your homophobic bullshit elsewhere." A few murmurs of assent and the arsehole flushed, taking on the look of a hunted animal.

"Whatever. It was just supposed to be a bit of a joke."

"Well, nobody's laughing, Matt." Dev said sharply. "I see your idea of what's funny hasn't developed since last term."

"Yeah, whatever." Beardy Guy — Matt — was done. "Come on, guys, let's hit the bar. We don't want to hang out here anyway." He glared at Ewan again. "Losers."

Ewan remained standing with Dev beside him until the three had gone. Then he let out a long breath and turned to Dev. "What the fuck was that about? You know him?"

Dev sighed, his face tense and unhappy. "Long story."

They sat down again, and Dev stirred his milkshake without speaking for little while. He glanced around at the other people in the café. They'd gone back to their own conversations now, and seemingly satisfied that nobody was listening, Dev looked at Ewan and said quietly, "I used to live on the same corridor as them in the halls of residence for my first two terms here."

"Fuck, really?" Ewan winced in sympathy. "That can't have been much fun."

"It wasn't. They took an instant dislike to me. I don't know why. I mean, I didn't do anything. They just knew I was different. At first it wasn't too bad. The usual nerd jokes, taking the piss out of me for actually going to classes and doing some work instead of going out to the bar every night and being too hungover to make it into lectures." He rolled his eyes. "And they used to talk about girls all the time—in the horrible, creepy way that some straight guys do. I made the mistake of calling them on it, and they were all 'oh come on, everyone talks about girls like that. What are you, a fucking queer?' So I told them that yes, I was gay, and that actually not all straight guys talk about girls like that, and that they were dickheads."

"Bloody hell, Dev," Ewan said in shocked admiration. "That was pretty brave."

"Brave, or stupid." Dev shrugged. "After that they were relentless. Harmless pranks at first, but annoying ones. Putting lube on my door handle, pouring salt into my milk in the communal kitchen, hiding my mail."

"Why didn't you report them to the warden?"

"I thought it would make them worse, and I hoped if I ignored them, they'd get bored and stop, eventually. But it just made them up their game."

"What happened?" The remainder of Ewan's danish pastry sat untouched on his plate, forgotten as he stared across the table at Dev.

"They broke into my room, found my stash of yaoi comics." He paused, face pained, and added quietly, "And my dildo. I was out at lectures, and when I got back, I found they'd taped pages of the comic — really graphic ones — to the outside of my door, and they'd stuck the dildo on there too, poking out like a coat hook. When I got back, a whole crowd was looking and laughing, people I didn't even know."

Ewan's stomach churned with a mixture of rage and nausea. "Fuck, Dev." Now it was his turn to reach across and take Dev's hand. He had to stop himself from squeezing so hard he would hurt him. The anger in his gut was hot lava. No wonder Dev had freaked out when Ewan had opened his parcel by mistake.

Dev looked up at him, his liquid brown eyes full of remembered pain and mortification. Ewan wanted to murder the bastards who'd hurt him.

"So." Dev took a deep breath and puffed out his cheeks as he exhaled. "There you have it. That's why I moved in next door to you. I couldn't stay in halls after that. I *did* report it then, but as I couldn't prove who'd broken into my room and... done what they did, there wasn't a lot the university could do. They offered to help me move to a different corridor, but luckily for me I knew this bloke, Rupert, who told me about the room where I am now. He assured me it was an LGBT-friendly house, so it seemed ideal." He gave Ewan a small hopeful smile. "And it's been good there so far. Mac and Jez are a couple, and Dani's really cool. Mike's okay as well. I'm not so keen on Shawn, but he's harmless enough. I feel safe there, and that's the main thing."

"And your neighbours are awesome," Ewan said, trying to lighten the mood.

It worked. Dev chuckled, and the sound soothed the fire in Ewan's belly. "Yeah, my neighbours are pretty great."

Dev laced his fingers with Ewan's, and they grinned at each other.

CHAPTER SEVEN

On Friday evening, Dev was in a state of extreme nervous excitement. He'd cleaned and tidied his room — even though there was barely anything out of place — and then showered, washing everything extra thoroughly in case things went in an unplanned direction.

His nerves made it hard for him to eat dinner, but the just-add-water instant-pasta thing he'd cooked wasn't very appetising anyway. He forced some of it down and put the rest in the fridge for the next day, before heading back upstairs to the bathroom he shared with Dani, the girl who had the other room on the top floor.

Dev brushed his teeth, and his stomach clenched with a delicious thrill of anticipation as he imagined kissing Ewan again and thought about what else they were going to do. He rinsed and spat, then checked his watch. Ten minutes to go, assuming Ewan was on time. God, Dev hoped he would be on time, or he might go crazy waiting.

He went back downstairs to wait. Jez and Mac were in the middle of a *Super Smash Bros.* battle in the living room, their faces scrunched with concentration as their on-screen characters punched and kicked and jumped on each other.

"You wanna play?" Jez asked without taking his eyes off the screen. "You can join in if you want. We can take turns or play a three-player game instead."

Normally, Dev would have said yes. He was into gaming, although he usually played more on his laptop than on a console, and it would have been a good opportunity to bond with his new housemates. "Thanks for the offer, but I can't tonight."

"Got plans?" Mac asked. "Oh, you fucker!" That was aimed at Jez who'd just kicked Mac's character high in the air and sent him plunging into an abyss.

"Yeah. Ewan from next door is coming over. To study," he added.

Jez and Mac's game was over, so they both turned to look at him. A blush heated Dev's cheeks.

"But you're not on the same course, are you? Isn't he a second year?" Mac frowned.

"Yes. He's studying psychology, but he needs help with statistics."

"Ugh, yeah. I get that," Jez said. "I'm lucky Mac can help me with that stuff. I'm crap at the maths side of things too."

"Yeah, well, you help me with the essays, so we're even." Mac bumped Jez's shoulder, and they exchanged a smile full of casual affection.

The doorbell rang and Dev jumped up. "That'll probably be him. Okay, have a good evening."

"Gaming and beer." Jez lifted his bottle and grinned at Dev. "It doesn't get much better than this."

"Have fun with the statistics," Mac called after Dev as he left the room.

"Thanks."

Dev's hand was sweaty with nerves, and he fumbled with the handle as he pulled the front door open. "Hi." He stood aside for Ewan. "Come in."

"Hi."

Ewan's smile made Dev's heart beat faster. Ewan was dressed casually in jeans and a hoodie with a zip down the front, and he had a bag slung on one shoulder.

Dev closed the door behind him. "After you." He gestured to the stairs.

Up in Dev's room, Ewan put his bag on Dev's bed and got out a folder and a textbook. "I don't have a particular stats assignment right now, but I thought maybe we can work through some of the chapters in this? I didn't do Maths A Level, so there's a lot of stuff I don't really get. I'm hoping you can help me make sense of it."

"Sure." Dev was glad to have a framework; it would be hard to tutor Ewan from scratch without some guidelines. "Have a seat."

"Oh, and I brought these too." Ewan got out a couple of cans of Coke. "I thought about bringing beer, but it probably wouldn't help my concentration. The caffeine will keep me awake. It's been a long week. Do you want one?"

"Yeah, thanks." Dev didn't like beer, anyway. He found it bitter and didn't understand the appeal at all. Coke was much nicer.

They settled down to work, and as Dev concentrated on figures, formulae, and graphs, his nerves faded. He knew where he was with numbers. They followed rules and were always predictable. He'd always loved the logic and pattern of mathematics. It was soothing, comforting almost, when the rest of the world didn't always make sense.

Working through a chapter on probability density function, Ewan appeared to be getting it. Occasionally he'd ask Dev to explain something twice or work through an example with him. But soon he was managing the problems on his own, and Dev felt a rush of satisfaction at seeing him take the concepts Dev had explained and apply them himself.

Dev was constantly aware of the warmth of Ewan beside him, the occasional brush of their elbows, or the touch of their knees under the desk. He liked the deep rumble of Ewan's voice and the sprinkle of reddish-brown hair on his wrist where he'd pushed his sleeve up.

The time flew past. Ewan was a fast learner and they worked through the whole chapter before stopping.

When Dev checked his clock and was surprised to see it was nine o'clock. "Do you want to start the next section?" he asked.

"No." Ewan pushed his chair back and yawned as he stretched. His hoodie rode up, taking his T-shirt with it. Dev's gaze latched onto the pale sliver of skin exposed and followed the line of hair that led down into Ewan's jeans. It was brighter than the hair on his arms, red like the hair on Ewan's head.

"Are you ready to get on with your lesson next?" Ewan's lazy drawl had a sexy edge to it.

Dev snapped his gaze back to Ewan's face and swallowed. "I think so." His voice came out a little squeaky.

Ewan grinned and raised his eyebrows.

Dev cleared his throat and tried to sound more sure. "Yes. Yes, I am."

Thrown back into nervous discomfort, Dev froze in his seat, unsure what Ewan expected of him.

Ewan pushed back his chair and stood, then offered his hand to Dev, who took it uncertainly.

Ewan pulled him up. "Don't look so scared. It'll be fun, I promise. Come on."

He led Dev to the bed, and they sat side-by-side. Ewan angled his body towards Dev and put his hand on Dev's shoulder, guiding him closer. "Can I kiss you?"

"Yeah," Dev managed, and with that all the air was sucked out of the room. Dev couldn't breathe. His heart hammered, his pulse a frantic drumbeat in his ears. He leaned in, putting a hand on Ewan's thigh to steady himself.

Ewan's lips were soft and dry, and the light stubble on his chin felt good where it brushed Dev's own. Ewan tasted sweet, like the Coke they'd been drinking, and when the kiss deepened, the inside of his mouth was hot and wet.

Dev had always thought kissing with tongues sounded kind of icky. But actually *doing* it was amazing, as though there was a direct line from his tongue to his groin. The slick movement of their mouths sent blood pumping southwards, filling his cock until it was hard and aching to be touched.

Desire made him forget his nerves. Needing to feel more of Ewan, he put a hand in Ewan's thick, wavy hair. Letting it slide through his fingers as he caressed Ewan's scalp with his fingertips. Ewan gave a low moan, and he tightened his fingers on Dev's jaw, angling his mouth to get deeper.

The sound Ewan made tore away the last of Dev's reservations, and Dev moaned too, a desperate noise that burst out of him without permission. He sounded like someone in a porn clip, but he didn't even care. Twisting around to try to get their bodies closer, Dev made Ewan lose his balance, and they fell back on the bed in a messy tangle.

Ewan broke the kiss, smiling. "Let's get a little more comfortable."

Dev let him move, wondering what Ewan had in mind. Ewan shuffled back to sit at the head of the bed, propped up on the pillows. "Come here."

Dev crawled towards him, uncertain.

Ewan guided him to sit astride his thighs. "Like this. Is that okay?"

Dev nodded, feeling shy again. His erection was obvious in his jeans, and as Ewan's gaze skimmed over it, another jolt of lust shot through him. He wondered if Ewan was hard—he hoped he was. Ewan certainly looked aroused, his cheeks flushed and his pupils huge as he dragged his gaze up to Dev's face again.

Ewan brought his hand up and touched Dev's lips lightly with the pad of his thumb. "You look hot with your lips all wet from my mouth. It makes me imagine how they'd look around my dick."

Dev let out a shuddery breath as he imagined that too. Not how they'd look, but how it would feel. How warm Ewan's skin would be under his tongue, how he'd taste. "I want that," he muttered.

"Me too. But not today. Today you're going to use your hand."

They stared at each other, the tension thick. Dev could feel every beat of his heart. "Now?"

"No time like the present." Ewan suddenly grinned, lightening the mood. He lifted his hips, his hardness bumping against Dev's arse. "Have at me."

Dev lifted up and moved back obediently. He adjusted himself first, tucking his dick into a more comfortable position. Then he unfastened Ewan's jeans, clumsy in his haste. Ewan helped him push them down just a little, so they were out of the way. Ewan's cock was a rigid bar, pushing against the stretchy material of his boxers. Dev hesitated before reaching out to run his fingers along the shaft. It flexed under his hand, and Ewan let out a huff of breath. Slowly, reverently almost, Dev lifted the waistband away and freed Ewan's erection. It reared up against his stomach, hard and perfect in its nest of neatly trimmed dark red pubes.

Another guy's dick finally in front of him for the taking, and Dev's mouth watered with the urge to kiss, lick, and suck. Even though it was all new to him, his instincts screamed at him to do all the things he'd fantasised about for years.

One step at a time.

Today was hand-job day, and as Dev wrapped his hand around Ewan's shaft and gave a tentative stroke, Ewan's gasp made this new experience thrilling enough.

Dev looked up at him, checking he was on the right track. Obviously, Dev had a dick of his own, but they were quite different. Ewan's was longer than Dev's, but slimmer, and he had a foreskin, unlike Dev. Dev had been circumcised as a baby, and he wasn't sure how different things would feel for Ewan. He pumped his hand carefully, rolling the skin back to expose the wet, red head of Ewan's dick. It looked almost raw compared to his. No wonder uncut guys were more sensitive. "Is that good?"

"Yeah," Ewan murmured. Then he bit his lip and stared at Dev intently, as though waiting for more.

"Tell me what you like." Dev presumed there was some personal preference involved even if the principle was the same. "What do you do when you're doing this for yourself?" He carried on stroking, steadily and a little faster.

"It depends what mood I'm in." Ewan's voice was husky as he replied. "If I'm in a hurry to get off, I'll go hard and fast. I don't bother with lube because I usually leak a lot anyway, especially when I'm close."

He was pretty sticky. Dev looked down. He stilled his hand and squeezed, watching as a bead of precome swelled in Ewan's slit. On the next upstroke, Dev caught it with his thumb and smeared it around the crown and over Ewan's frenulum.

"Fuck," Ewan jerked.

"Too much?"

"Not if you want to make me come fast." Ewan's voice was rough. He swallowed. "It depends how much practice you think you need. You're doing pretty well from where I'm sitting."

"How do you get yourself off if you're not in a hurry?" Dev slowed his strokes right down, gripping gently and moving his hand in an almost imperceptible slide. Although his own cock was getting pretty desperate for some attention, he didn't want to rush things. He wanted to learn as much as he could.

"Jesus, you like the dirty talk, then? You're pretty kinky for a virgin."

"I wasn't trying to talk dirty. I just want to know what you like."

Ewan chuckled breathlessly. "Somehow that only makes it hotter."

Dev stored that piece of information away for future reference. It was good to know talking turned Ewan on, because Dev always had a lot of questions. There was so much he wanted to know. "So tell me, then."

"Okay… well. Sometimes I don't even touch my dick much at first. I might give it a quick tug to make it hard. But then I stop and focus on other things. My nipples are really sensitive, so I like to stroke those, or pinch them."

Dev let his gaze drop to Ewan's chest. His hoodie was too thick for Dev to be able to see whether Ewan's nipples were hard like his cock. "Can I do that?"

"Fuck yes. Here, let me…." Ewan unzipped his hoodie and leaned forward to shrug it off. "My T-shirt too?"

"Yes — if you want?"

Ewan answered by stripping it off in one swift movement, flashing dark red armpit hair at Dev as he pulled it over his head. His torso was muscled, but lean rather than bulky. A light dusting of hair covered his chest, and cinnamon freckles sprinkled his wide shoulders. He was lovely to look at.

Dev's gaze settled on Ewan's pale pink nipples. They stuck out as though he was cold, and when Dev reached out a tentative fingertip to touch one, it got harder as he rubbed it. "Like that?"

"Yeah," Ewan said, his voice a little rough. "You could use your mouth on them too, if you want. I like it when guys do that."

The thought of nameless, faceless guys licking Ewan's nipples sent a sharp rush of jealousy through Dev, which was ridiculous. He had no claim on Ewan. But not wanting to be outdone, he shuffled back and lowered his face to Ewan's chest. The hair tickled his lips, and the rich, masculine scent of Ewan's skin made his balls tingle. He gave one of Ewan's nipples a tentative lick as he rubbed his fingers over the other one, and Ewan hummed.

"Feels good," Ewan said. "Keep going."

Dev licked again, then sucked the little nub between his lips as he pinched the other lightly.

"Fuck yes, like that."

Dev carried on for a little while, and Ewan started to make more and more desperate-sounding noises. Occasionally he'd curse or mutter Dev's name. It was fucking hot.

"I'm getting close now," Ewan gasped. "Jerk me off again." Dev wrapped his right hand around Ewan's shaft and started to stroke. "Faster. And touch my balls with your other hand."

Dev reached down. Ewan's sac had drawn up tight. Dev cupped and squeezed it gently. Ewan's whole body was tense as he strained towards climax. He had his hands on Dev's arse now, fingers tensing and releasing reflexively as he panted in shuddery breaths.

"Oh God... yeah... yeah, *fuck!*"

The last word was loud, and Dev was glad Dani was away for the weekend, or she'd have heard it through the wall.

Dev watched as come shot from Ewan's cock, painting his stomach and Dev's fist with white streaks. Dev carried on stroking him through it, the grip of his hand wet and slippery with Ewan's spunk, the scent of it strong.

Ewan put his hands on Dev's face and pulled him in for a hot, hungry kiss. He panted into Dev's mouth, wet and messy, and Dev loved it. He loved that he'd made Ewan fall apart like that. He felt powerful, and sexy. It was a new feeling for Dev, and an awesome one.

When Ewan finally pulled away, he smiled. "That was really good."

"Yeah?" Dev smiled back.

"Yes. You get full marks on your hand-job module, with bonus points for nipple play." There was a pause, and Ewan's gaze dropped to Dev's crotch. "Now it's your turn. I think you earned it." He started to undo Dev's fly.

Dev watched Ewan's fingers as he deftly unfastened the button and then the zip. The fly fell open to show Dev's bulge. Wetness bloomed at the tip, dark and obvious on his pale grey boxer briefs. Ewan traced the sticky patch with a fingertip, sending an electric jolt to Dev's balls and the base of his spine. Heat pooled in his groin and his breath caught.

"That's so hot," Ewan murmured. "I love how turned on you are, just from getting me off." He tugged Dev's underwear down below his balls. "Oh wow, you're cut." He took Dev's cock in his hand and stroked lightly. "I've never played with a cut dick before. You'll have to tell me what feels good for you, because I've read it's a little different." He traced his finger around the crown, and then around the circumcision scar where the skin changed colour.

Dev shivered at his touch. It was so strange—and wonderful—to have someone else's hand on his dick. Then Ewan stroked his balls, cupping and squeezing lightly. They were heavy and full, and God, he was desperate to come.

"You're not cut here." Ewan's voice was soft and teasing as he ran his fingers through the thick thatch of dark hair at Dev's groin.

Dev flushed hot. "Sorry. I should have—"

"I like it." Ewan ran his other hand over Dev's stomach and chest. "The contrast with how smooth you are everywhere else is really sexy."

Ewan's hand was on Dev's cock again, pumping him in steady strokes. The friction was good.

"It's really different." Ewan's brow furrowed in concentration as he watched his hand. "There isn't as much skin to slide around. Does that feel okay? Do you want some lube or lotion or something?"

"It's good," Dev managed breathlessly. "But with lube it's even better. Let me get it."

He reached over to the drawer by the bed. "Here."

Ewan took the bottle and squirted some into his palm before taking hold of Dev again. "You've got a gorgeous cock," he said, stroking with not quite enough pressure. "I love guessing what a guy's dick will look like hard before I see it. I'm usually pretty good at predicting. Hah! Pre-*dick*-ting. It's my superpower. But I was wrong about yours."

"You didn't think it would be gorgeous?" Dev was worried now. Did he give off ugly-dick vibes or something?

Ewan laughed. "It's not that. I just thought it would be slimmer, more in proportion with the rest of you. It's a pleasant surprise how thick it is."

"It's not very long, though." Dev gasped as Ewan tightened his grip. "Yours is at least an inch longer."

"Give me girth any day." Ewan stroked him harder and faster, and Dev groaned, bucking into the movement. He put his hands on Ewan's shoulders to support himself. Ewan felt firm and strong under his palms. "You like that? Good." Ewan carried on. "Your dick is really nice and fat. It would feel amazing to be fucked by you."

Dev closed his eyes, a mental image of Ewan on all fours on Dev's bed, spread open for Dev's cock. "Fuck," he gasped. "More… do it harder."

Ewan obliged, moving his hand just right and giving Dev what he needed. Dev opened his eyes again in time to watch as he cried out and came all over Ewan, who kept stroking him until he was done.

"Good?" Ewan asked, a lazy smile on his face.

"Mmph." Dev couldn't form words. He blinked at Ewan stupidly, surprised his glasses weren't steamed up.

Ewan curled his free hand around the nape of Dev's neck and tugged him down for one last kiss. Soft and gentle now, and Dev felt the sweetness of it in his chest like a burst of warmth.

After they'd cleaned themselves up and put their dicks away, Ewan packed up his books. "So, uh, I guess I'd better go." He stood by the desk with his bag in his hand.

Disappointment stabbed at Dev. But what had he expected? Cuddling? That wasn't on the list of things to practice. He found himself wishing it was. "Okay." He shrugged.

Ewan stared at him intently, but Dev wasn't sure what he was looking for.

"Thank you," Dev said. It came out sounding inappropriately formal, and his voice was tight in his throat. For all the reading about social interaction Dev had done, he'd never found a guide for how to behave after a sex lesson. "That was very…." He scrabbled around for a word to complete the phrase. Maybe he should have stopped at "thank you."

"Educational?" Ewan's lips curved and his eyes were bright with mischief. "Informative…?" His grin turned dirty. "Hot?"

Dev grinned too. Ewan had a magical ability to put him at ease. He'd never known anyone quite like him before. "All of the above."

"I should have made an evaluation form for you to fill in at the end of each session."

Dev could tell from his tone that Ewan was still joking. "Yes. And I could make you one for the maths lessons."

"That was also awesome, by the way. I forgot to say earlier because I got distracted by the orgasms… but you're a good teacher. Thank you."

"So are you." Dev flushed, remembering Ewan's instructions earlier.

"Next week, then?" Ewan asked. "Blow jobs 101?" Dev nodded, not trusting his voice to come out as anything other than a hoarse squeak. "Friday night?"

Dev managed to speak that time. "Yeah, probably. I'll text you to confirm."

"Okay."

Dev followed Ewan down the stairs, feeling like he ought to see him out. They paused at the front door.

"Bye, then," Ewan said.

Dev pushed his hair out of his eyes to give him something to do with his hands, which unaccountably itched to touch Ewan again. "Bye, thanks again."

Ewan gave Dev one of his hundred-watt grins. "It really was my pleasure." And then he opened the door and went.

Dev closed it behind him with a quiet click. Standing in the hall, his body still buzzing and his mind whirling with everything that had happened, a sound drifted in from the living room—Mac and Jez playing *Mario Kart*, judging by the sound of the music.

Needing a distraction from the thoughts crowding his head, Dev went to join them. "Hi, can I play?"

"Sure, after this race," Jez replied without taking his gaze off the screen.

"Did you have a good evening studying with Ewan?" Mac asked.

"Yes," Dev said, glad they weren't looking at him. Because he couldn't have stopped the smile that spread over his face if he'd tried. "It was *very* good, thanks."

CHAPTER EIGHT

Although Dev was often at the edges of Ewan's thoughts during the next week, Ewan didn't have to time to do more than fantasise about him when he jerked off in the shower or in bed late at night.

He kept a lookout for Dev when leaving the house or arriving back, hoping he might run into him in the street, but their schedules didn't match and there was no sign of him. Though Ewan did see Mac a couple of times, who greeted him with a friendly grin. Once he saw Mac with the blond guy who also lived next door, walking down the road hand in hand. The sight of them together hit Ewan with an unexpected lurch of envy. For the past year or so, he hadn't missed being in a relationship at all, happy enough with the freedom of casual sex and no-strings hook-ups. So why was he suddenly looking at Mac and that other guy and wishing he had a boyfriend again?

Ewan had an essay deadline on Friday and had to stay up late on Thursday to get it finished. Of course, then he was so knackered he slept through his alarm, woke at ten, and missed a class with the tutor the essay was meant for. He ran all the way to campus, arriving sweaty and apologetic at her office.

"I'm really sorry, Dr Jeffreys," he panted, holding out the printed essay. "I finished it, but I didn't make your class this morning." He winced. She was pretty strict about attendance.

To his surprise, she frowned sympathetically. "You look rough, do you have a temperature?"

"Um—" He mopped at the sweat on his brow; his face was probably flushed from running. "—I'm not sure. Maybe?"

She took the essay and backed away quickly. "Well, thank you for bringing this in. Get well soon."

"Thanks." Ewan turned away quickly to hide his grin and faked a cough.

Dodged a bullet.

His phone chimed when he was in the library later, searching the shelves for some books for the next essay he needed to research. He quickly pulled it out and turned the ringer off so he wouldn't disturb people more than he already had.

Hi, I hope you had a good week. I'm just checking we're still on for tonight?

Ewan smiled. He loved the way Dev always typed his texts in full sentences, never mind full words. It was so typical of him.

Yep, definitely. Where and when? Ewan replied.

My place again, if that suits you. And how about 7.30?

Fine, see you then.

Ewan would normally have shortened that to *CU*, but he didn't want Dev to judge him. Another text arrived from Dev before Ewan put his phone away.

Did you get your test results yet?
Yes, all negative.
Me too.

Fuck being judged—that was an emoji moment. He sent two of those aubergines that looked like dicks, followed by water droplets.

Dev took a little while to reply, but when the message finally popped up, it was a picture of a tongue sticking out.

Ewan stifled a snort of laughter, put his phone back in his pocket, and carried on searching through the books on cognitive therapy.

When Ewan rang the bell at Dev's place that evening, it was the blond guy — Mac's boyfriend — who answered it.

"Oh, hey." The guy grinned. "It's Ewan, isn't it? Come in. You're here to see Dev, yeah? He's in the kitchen."

"Yeah, hi. Um…." Ewan couldn't remember his name.

"Jez."

"Hi, Jez."

Ewan followed him down the hallway and into the brightly lit kitchen. It was hot in there; the windows had steamed up, and there was an alarming smell of burning.

Mac was stirring something in a wok, and Dev was scraping at a pan in the sink.

"Dev, do you want me to stir this for you?" Mac asked. "I think it's sticking."

"Oh no, not again!" Dev turned. His cheeks were pink and his hair was rumpled. "Oh." His face registered surprise when he caught sight of Ewan. "Didn't you get my text?"

"No." Ewan's heart sank. Had Dev tried to cancel on him?

That hurt more than he would have expected. He'd rushed to get there on time because he'd been looking forward to it. He pulled his phone out, and there was Dev's message.

Sorry, I'm running late, can you come round at 8 instead?

Relief rippled through him. "Ah. Yeah, now I got it. Sorry, I put my phone on silent earlier and forgot to put the sound back on."

"Dev, this is definitely sticking," Mac said. "You're going to fuck up another pan at this rate. I'm turning it down."

"Can I help?" Ewan asked.

Mac spoke over Dev's protests. "I think he needs it. Keep an eye on this for him." He pointed to a pan of something unidentifiable that was bubbling away like crazy in a saucepan, then turned to Jez. "Ours is done now, babe. Can you get bowls out?"

Mac had made some sort of stir-fry with vegetables, noodles, and what looked like chicken. It was way more appealing than whatever Dev was cooking.

"What the hell is this, Dev?" Ewan asked as he poked the dodgy stuff in the pan.

"Baked beans, frozen peas, and chopped-up frankfurters — veggie ones."

Ewan wrinkled his nose. "Um… is that a family recipe or what?"

"It's what I had left after I burned the sauce I was heating up for pasta," Dev explained. "It contains all the major food groups."

"Huh." Ewan poked it again. It looked truly disgusting.

"Are you hungry? Because I think there's enough if you'd like some."

"Ah. No… no," Ewan said hastily. "I'm fine, thank you."

Jez snorted. "You see, Dev. I told you no normal person would eat that shit. Just look at it!"

Dev had finished scraping the burned mess out of the pan. He came over and took the spoon from Ewan. "It might taste better than it looks."

Ewan had to admire his optimism.

Jez shook his head in mock sympathy. "Let's hope so. Hey, Ewan, do you know how to cook?"

"Yeah, I like cooking. Why?"

"Well… Dev's helping you with maths, isn't he? Maybe it would be fair exchange if you took this boy in hand and taught him how to cook before he burns our house down. He's a fucking disaster."

Ewan nearly choked at Jez's turn of phrase. He was already looking forward to taking Dev in hand again later—and in his mouth. He cleared his throat. "Um. Maybe?" He glanced at Dev, uncertain how to respond.

"But Ewan's already—" Dev began.

"Yeah, that's a great idea, actually." Ewan cut in. He had no idea what the hell Dev had been about to say and didn't want to find out. "I could do that, if you want?" He raised his eyebrows at Dev.

Dev blinked and then pushed his glasses up the bridge of his nose. It was a nervous habit; they hadn't actually slipped, but Dev often did it when he was thinking.

"Okay." Dev shrugged.

Mac finished tipping out the delicious looking stir-fry into his and Jez's bowls. Dev looked enviously at it as the fragrant steam rose.

"Okay, we'll leave you to it." Jez picked up his bowl and some cutlery. "We're gonna go and eat in the living room."

He and Mac took their food and left.

"You don't have to teach me to cook, you know," Dev said as soon as they'd gone. "We already had an arrangement."

"I don't mind."

Dev frowned. "We could do extra maths to make up for it, two sessions a week instead of one?"

Ewan briefly considered it. More time with Dev was appealing. But doing maths wasn't how he wanted to spend that extra time. "No, seriously it's fine. I cook for myself most nights anyway. You can come over and help me sometimes, and learn as you go. We can go halves on the ingredients. It's more fun cooking for two people."

The furrows in Dev's brow ironed out, and a small smile tugged at his lips. "Okay, then." He stirred the food in the pan again. "I've been meaning to look up some recipes to try, but I haven't got round to it yet."

"Well, have a look this weekend, and let me know the sort of things you'd like to learn to cook, and we can work it out."

Dev added some cooked pasta to the mess in the pan and stirred that in too. It didn't improve the appearance much. Once he'd dished up his weird concoction, he asked, "Can we go to the living room while I eat? They'll be watching TV."

"Okay."

Sure enough, Mac and Jez were partway through an episode of *Breaking Bad*.

"Oh, I love this show." Ewan sat down on the spare sofa, and Dev took a seat beside him.

"It's fucking awesome, isn't it?" Mac said in agreement.

Dev ate as they watched. The scent of his dinner wafted towards Ewan. It didn't smell as bad as it looked. He glanced sideways at Dev, who was chewing, his gaze fixed on the television. Dev's throat bobbed as he swallowed. He had a long, smooth neck and a pronounced Adam's apple. Clean-shaven as always, there was just the lightest shadow of stubble on his chin and above his upper lip.

"Do you want to try some?" Dev asked. He raised his eyebrows, brown eyes amused behind his glasses.

Ewan had been caught staring. It wasn't the food that had captured his attention, though. "Oh, go on, then. I'd be lying if I said I wasn't intrigued."

"It's really not that bad."

Dev offered him a forkful. Ewan parted his lips. Their gazes locked, and Dev's hand wobbled. Warm sauce dripped onto Ewan's lip and down his chin.

"Sorry," Dev said.

Ewan chewed. It was better than he'd expected. A bit bland, but not offensive.

"It would be better with melted cheese on top." He caught the sauce from his chin with his finger and licked that clean.

Dev was still watching him, his eyes darker than usual. Ewan was a little more thorough with the finger-licking than was strictly necessary. He liked the way Dev's eyes followed the movement of his tongue and lingered on his lips.

"Do you need us to leave you guys alone?"

Jez's voice made Ewan jump with a guilty start. Both Jez and Mac were watching them, with matching knowing grins.

"What? I spilled some." Ewan put on his best innocent expression.

"Of course you did." Jez smirked and turned his attention back to the TV.

When Ewan looked back at Dev, Dev had flushed, but he gave Ewan a small, private smile that made Ewan's stomach give a happy swoop.

CHAPTER NINE

That evening, Ewan would have happily skipped the statistics and gone straight to the blow jobs, but Dev took his role as maths tutor very seriously. He made Ewan work through another whole chapter—on *t*-tests this time—and solve several problems to prove he'd understood what he'd learned.

"Reading the theory is never enough," Dev said when Ewan complained he'd got it and didn't need to do more example questions. "You only consolidate your learning through putting it into practice."

Ewan huffed and grumbled his way through three more problems before Dev was satisfied. He had to admit, Dev was right. By the time he'd finished, he really had got the hang of it, and it felt as if the new knowledge would stick.

"Okay?" he asked when Dev checked his working.

"Perfect."

"In that case, it's time for *your* lesson." Ewan's groin tingled with anticipation. "How do you want to do this?"

"What do you mean?"

"Do you want me to suck you first, to show you how it's done? Or do you want to have a go, and I can tell you what I like? We could try both at the same time if we lie on the bed... but I think it would be easier for you to concentrate if we take turns rather than sixty-nineing."

Dev swallowed, and the lovely, graceful bob of his throat caught Ewan's attention again. Ewan wanted to kiss him there, to feel that movement under his lips and tongue.

"Can I go first?" Dev asked. "I mean… I want to suck you first." There was tension written in the lines of his shoulders and the set of his jaw.

Ewan took his hand. Dev's palm was warm and damp. "Are you sure?" Dev nodded. "Come here." Ewan tugged on Dev's hand until he stood, and Ewan pushed back the chair he was sitting in. He guided Dev to straddle his thighs, his hands firm on Dev's slim hips.

Dev put his hands on Ewan's shoulders. "I can't suck your cock like this."

"I know. I want to kiss you first."

Some kissing might help to relieve Dev's nervousness, but Ewan wanted the kiss for himself too. He brought a hand up to Dev's face. "Can you take these off?" He tapped the thick black frame of Dev's glasses with a fingertip.

"Oh yeah. Of course." Dev took them off and put them on the desk. He blinked. He looked weirdly vulnerable without them on. "I feel naked now."

Ewan chuckled. "Well, I have to tell you, you're still overdressed. Come here."

He slid his hands into Dev's hair and guided him down into a slow, thorough kiss. The tension in Dev's body disappeared at the first touch of their tongues and he melted into Ewan, one hand curling into Ewan's hair as the other brushed over his chest, teasing a nipple through his T-shirt.

Someone has a good memory for details.

For a beginner, Dev was really great at kissing when he let himself go. He was a little messy, a little overenthusiastic perhaps, but that was part of what Ewan liked about it. Knowing he was Dev's first, that this was all knew to him, was a massive turn-on. It made Ewan feel special, even if he was really just convenient.

When they parted, they were both breathing hard. Sweat prickled on Ewan's back, so he took his T-shirt off. "Yours too?"

Dev obliged, revealing the long lean stretch of his torso as he pulled the shirt over his head. Ewan ran his hands over Dev's stomach and chest, making him shiver.

"So, can I suck you now?" Dev asked.

Ewan's cock throbbed.

Yes please.

But Dev's eagerness made a wicked part of Ewan want to tease, even if it would be torture for him too.

He touched Dev's wet lips with two fingers. "Suck these first. Show me what you want to do to me."

Dev's gaze widened in surprise, and Ewan thought he might refuse. But then he opened his mouth so Ewan's fingertips slid inside, and Ewan's brain short-circuited at the first swipe of Dev's tongue.

He gasped.

That seemed to give Dev confidence, because he took hold of Ewan's hand to guide it and then sucked his fingers in slowly and steadily. Past the first knuckle, past the second, and all the way until there was nothing more to take.

"Fuck," Ewan muttered.

The inside of Dev's mouth was hot and sleek, and as he drew back, he stroked the underside of Ewan's fingers with his tongue. Dev repeated the movement a few times, and each time Ewan's fingers got wetter and his jeans got tighter. Dev watched him intently as he sucked, and that only made it hotter. He took everything so seriously.

A lot of guys would have laughed, or been embarrassed about doing this, or told Ewan to stop messing around and get his cock out. But Dev did exactly what Ewan asked of him. His obedience and his eagerness to please satisfied a part of Ewan he hadn't known existed before. Sure, he was usually pretty bossy in bed. He liked to be in charge and had never been afraid of saying what he wanted. But this was different. This was new for him too.

Dev finally released Ewan's fingers with a wet sound. His cheeks were flushed, and when Ewan looked down at Dev's lap, the sweatpants Dev was wearing today did nothing to conceal his erection. He was as into it as Ewan was.

"You want to try my cock now?" Ewan sensed Dev was waiting for permission. Dev nodded eagerly. "Go on, then."

Dev dropped to his knees between Ewan's parted legs. Ewan was wearing jeans and his dick was obvious, trapped against his hip. Dev pressed his lips to it through the thick fabric, following the line of the shaft up to the tip.

"You gonna make me beg for it?" Ewan asked hoarsely. "Or do you want me to make you take it?"

Dev moaned and tightened his fingers on Ewan's thighs where he gripped them.

"Come on, then." Ewan unfastened his jeans. He raised his hips so he could push them down along with his boxers. "Help me get these off."

Dev pulled them down, freeing Ewan's feet carefully so that he could spread his legs wide again. Dev, still wearing his sweatpants but nothing else, settled back on his knees in front of him. He looked up, cheeks flushed and lips parted.

Ewan gripped his shaft and angled the head towards Dev's mouth. "Suck it. Like you did my fingers."

Dev did exactly that. And if his mouth had felt good on Ewan's fingers, it was nothing compared to how it felt around his cock.

"Oh Jesus," Ewan groaned.

Dev was cautious at first, only sucking down what he could manage, but soon he got bold. He took Ewan deep and then gagged as Ewan bumped the back of his throat. He drew off with his eyes watering, muttering, "Sorry, sorry."

"Hey, it's fine." Ewan touched his cheek. "You're getting ambitious. Just do what feels okay for you. It's all good for me."

Dev gave one of his sweet smiles and took Ewan's cock in his hand. He held it at the base as he sucked again, this time only going about halfway with his mouth and using his hand for the rest.

"Yeah, that's good. That's really good."

Each downstroke of Dev's hand drew Ewan's foreskin back, and Dev's lips slipped over his exposed crown, sending sparks of tingling sensation to Ewan's balls and arse. He clenched his muscles, feeling his sac draw up tight. "I'm getting close now," he warned Dev. "Unless you slow down and change things up, I'm going to come soon."

Dev drew back, leaving a sticky trail of precome connecting them. He broke it with his finger and chuckled when it dripped down his chin.

Ewan's cock bobbed, straining for more as the cooler air hit his sensitive skin.

"What else do you like?" Dev's voice was husky.

From sucking my cock. Ewan's toes curled. *I did that.*

"You could, uh, lick my balls, maybe? That always feels good, but it won't make me come."

"Okay." Dev buried his face in Ewan's groin, all hot breath and eager tongue. "You smell really good here," he muttered.

Ewan made a choked sound.

Dev stopped what he was doing and looked up. "Sorry, was that a weird thing to say? But I have a really good sense of smell, so I always notice scents."

"No, it's not weird. It's hot when you say those things. It takes me by surprise, that's all." He put a hand on Dev's head and gently guided his mouth back where he wanted it. "You look at me, all innocent puppy eyes, and then come out with dirty things like that. It's awesome."

Dev grinned before getting back to licking.

He drove Ewan crazy with soft swipes of his tongue and totally ignored Ewan's cock, but Ewan's erection didn't flag in the slightest. He came off the boil just enough to enjoy Dev's ministrations without being afraid of coming, but it was going to be game over really soon when Dev got his mouth back on Ewan's cock.

Eventually, Ewan couldn't wait anymore. Plus he reckoned Dev deserved a turn in the hot seat. "Suck my cock again. I want you to make me come."

Dev went back to it as if he was starving for it, sucking on the head and swirling his tongue around to catch all the precome that had leaked out.

Ewan threaded his fingers into the thick silk of Dev's hair. "It's not going to take long. Do you want me to come in your mouth?" He was breathless, his voice tight and strained.

Dev flicked his gaze up and nodded, tightening his lips around Ewan's cock.

"Fuck, okay. Don't stop, then. Like that."

Dev focused more on the tip, using his tongue on the underside, and Ewan was nearly there. Pleasure spiralled through him, tightening his muscles as he tried to fight the urge to thrust into the wet heat of Dev's mouth.

"God, Dev… *yeah.*" The last word was a strangled cry and he tensed, coming in a dizzying rush of pure sensation.

Dev choked but didn't pull off, sucking Ewan through it until Ewan pushed him gently away, shaken and oversensitive.

Only then did Dev swallow. His nose wrinkled a little. "It's more bitter than mine usually is."

Ewan huffed a breathless laugh. "Do you often eat your own come? I guess it's a good source of protein, and I know you like your food groups."

"No, but I've tasted it a few times. I was curious." Dev's reply was utterly serious.

Ewan wasn't even surprised. He was getting used to Dev now. He smiled. "Of course you were. Now get up here." He guided Dev back into his lap and gave him a filthy kiss, licking into Dev's mouth to taste his own release on Dev's tongue.

Dev moaned, rocking his erection against Ewan's stomach.

Ewan kissed his way down Dev's jaw to the soft skin of his neck. He breathed in the scent of Dev's skin and tasted his sweat, then slipped his hand into Dev's sweats and curled his fingers around wet, eager hardness. "Commando... nice."

Dev made a high, desperate sound at the touch of Ewan's hand and thrust into his grip.

"Steady." Ewan pressed more soft kisses to Dev's throat. Dev's pulse fluttered wildly against his lips. He gripped him tightly, refusing to stroke. "Calm down a bit, yeah?"

Dev swallowed. "I'm trying."

"Let's swap places. It's your turn to be sucked. You earned it."

"Yeah?" Dev asked as he climbed off Ewan's lap.

"Yeah. You were amazing." Ewan stood. "Let's get these off." He pushed down Dev's sweatpants, freeing his cock, and then he knelt to get them off completely.

When Dev was naked, Ewan looked up from his position at Dev's feet. Dev's body was lean beauty and angled grace. His cock reared up, thick and eager.

Ewan put firm hands on Dev's hips and buried his face in Dev's thick pubes. He inhaled musk and spice and sex. Dev's cock jerked hot against his cheek. "You smell good here too," Ewan said.

Slowly, teasingly, he turned his head and watched Dev as he licked a slow, teasing stripe along the side of his cock. When he reached the tip, he closed his lips around it and sucked lightly, tasting the salty sweetness of precome.

Dev's legs wobbled and he let out a gasp.

Ewan released him and grinned. "Sit down."

Dev sat, and Ewan knelt again. He ran his hands up Dev's thighs, the prickle of hair making his palms tingle. He pushed Dev's legs wide and paused to admire him for a moment. Dev's cock rose against his flat stomach, his balls high and tight beneath. He was a beautiful sight in the angled light from the desk lamp.

Dev's arms hung by his sides, but his clenched fists gave away his tension. Dev rasped, "What are you waiting for?"

"A little anticipation only makes it better when you finally get it." Ewan's mouth watered and he licked his lips. It wasn't only Dev he was torturing by making him wait. The tension was getting to him too, his cock already thickening and lengthening again at the sight of Dev spread out and waiting for his mouth.

Ewan started with Dev's balls, licking and nuzzling them, feeling the texture of Dev's skin and hair against his lips and tongue. Of course he got a pube stuck somewhere in his mouth. He tried to ignore it at first, but he worried it was going to end up in his throat. "Sorry, hang on a sec."

Ewan pulled away and reached into his mouth with a finger to catch the hair lodged somewhere on the roof of his mouth. "There. Got it!"

"Is that why you cut yours?" Dev asked. "Maybe I should too."

"It's one of the reasons. I only trim, though. I don't shave it all off. I like some hair down there."

"What do you use?"

"Little clippers, like a beard trimmer." Dev's cock had flagged a bit. It really wasn't the best time to discuss personal grooming habits, but maybe a pause wasn't a bad thing. Dev had looked as though he was close to coming before. "Anyway, where were we?"

Ewan turned his attention back to Dev's cock. After licking his lips to make them wet, he pressed them gently against the tip, parting them around the head until the crown popped into his mouth. He sucked lightly, circling his tongue a few times. Dev hissed in a breath, tensing his thighs.

Ewan pulled off to ask, "Is that good? Or am I being too gentle? I'm used to a foreskin, so tell me what's going to get you off."

"Just watching you suck me will probably get me off." Dev stared at his mouth. "But you could do it a little harder."

Ewan was learning as much as Dev was. It made sense that Dev would like it a bit rougher than he did. The head was probably less sensitive — he'd read that somewhere.

He sucked on the head again, using his tongue to try and give more stimulation and make up for Dev's lack of foreskin. He watched Dev, trying to read his reactions. Dev gasped again and made a sound of appreciation as Ewan used his tongue on the underside. "That's good. That bit underneath is really sensitive — where the head joins the shaft."

Ewan held Dev's cock in his hand and stroked him as he sucked. There wasn't much movement of the skin, not like Ewan was used to, but he could slide it up and down a little. Dev seemed to be enjoying it anyway, if the dazed expression on his face was anything to go by.

Dev brought his hand up to cup Ewan's jaw, watching intently where his cock slid in and out of Ewan's mouth, the head popping past Ewan's lips with each suck. "Yeah. That's good. Fuck, Ewan…." His voice was strained and tense.

Ewan sucked faster, moving his hand a little more. Dev's cock was wet with his spit and his hand slid more easily now.

Dev groaned. "Oh—I'm going to come."

As soon as he said the words, his cock pulsed and Ewan tasted the warm salt of his release.

Dev panted, his abs clenching as he filled Ewan's mouth.

When Ewan finished licking him clean, he looked up at Dev, who was watching him.

"That was amazing," Dev said, sounding raw and shaken, as if the pieces of him had been rearranged.

Ewan felt a powerful urge to kiss him, to hold him. But would Dev want it now that the sex part of the evening was over? Ewan wasn't ready for their connection to end, so he stood up and took Dev's hand. "Come here. My knees are sore from the floor."

Dev went willingly, allowing Ewan to pull him down onto the bed.

CHAPTER TEN

Dev lay on his back, still feeling slightly dazed as Ewan settled beside him and pulled the duvet up. Dev tensed as Ewan moved closer, unsure of what was expected of him. "What are we doing now?"

"What does it look like?" Ewan put his arm across Dev's chest and kissed his cheek.

It was intimate but not sexual, and Dev was confused because that was more than he'd expected to get from Ewan. He wasn't complaining. It was good to be close to Ewan, but unnerving too. Ewan made Dev feel things he hadn't anticipated when they agreed to the arrangement, which was supposed to be just about sex, about Dev getting experience. Once they were done, Ewan would go back to hooking up with other guys and Dev would be ready to do the same.

That was what he'd wanted, wasn't it? To get some experience so he'd be confident enough to date guys and to eventually find a boyfriend.

Only, with Ewan lying beside him, stroking Dev's chest, his breath warm on Dev's cheek, maybe Dev had already found what he wanted.

But Ewan wasn't looking for a relationship; he'd made that clear at the start.

"How come you don't have a boyfriend?" Dev's heart thumped as he asked the question. "Not that it's any of my business, but I was wondering."

"Me and my ex ended things when I came to uni. We didn't want a long-distance relationship.

And I was ready to play the field anyway. I didn't get much chance to do that before, living at home with my parents. It's been fun being young, free, and single."

Dev's heart twisted in a way that was new to him. "Oh. Yeah. I guess it would be. I suppose I'll find out soon."

"Yeah. Once you're ready to graduate from the Ewan Campbell School of Sex."

Ewan's voice was light, but he turned away to lie on his back beside Dev so they were no longer touching, and Dev missed the warmth of his skin. Did Ewan mean it as a joke? Dev wasn't sure because Ewan hadn't sounded very amused.

Something had soured between them, and Dev didn't know what he'd done wrong. Wanting to fix things, he rolled onto his side and reached tentatively for Ewan. He stroked Ewan's chest in silence, enjoying the soft hair and the delicious sensation of Ewan's nipples tightening under his fingertips.

Ewan didn't respond at first, but he didn't try to stop him. Feeling bolder, Dev propped himself up on an elbow and kissed Ewan's shoulder, then his neck, then his jaw.

Ewan turned his face to meet Dev and they found each other's mouths. Heat built between them again, slower this time, but inevitable. It was so much easier when they let their bodies do the talking. There was no misunderstanding when it came to this simple, physical desire. Dev might still lack confidence, but when he gave himself up to it, his body knew what to do even when intellect failed him. He pushed all thoughts away and let instinct take over.

Ewan moaned into Dev's mouth and put strong arms around him. Dev shifted so he was on top of Ewan, kneeling astride him, their bodies aligned from groin to chest. They kissed. Messy, desperate kisses and Ewan was hard again—just like Dev.

"Yeah," Ewan gasped, half into Dev's mouth. He put his hands on Dev's arse and encouraged the small movements he was already making. "Harder."

Dev broke the kiss so he could focus. He propped himself up on his elbows and thrust against Ewan, their cocks sliding together, their sweat and precome easing the way. It was all heat and desire, touch and the scent of sex, even the sounds they made sent Dev closer to the edge. Their ragged breathing and the rhythmic creak of the bed made it sound as if they were fucking. Dev fleetingly wondered whether Dani was in her room, and if she was, whether she could hear them, but then Ewan reached between them and took both their cocks in his hand, squeezing and stroking, and Dev stopped caring about anything other than the overwhelming need to come.

Ewan beat him to it, shooting hot and wet. His come slicked the way for Dev, like lube, only warmer and dirtier—in a good way.

Ewan carried on stroking, his hand slippery as Dev fucked into his fist. "Come on," Ewan muttered, "So fucking sexy, I want you to come all over me."

Dev gasped at the words and promptly obliged. "Fuck," he hissed, cock pulsing in Ewan's grip.

"Yeah." Ewan jerked him through it until Dev was done, and then he pulled Dev's head down with his clean hand so they could kiss again.

When they finally separated, Ewan said, "That was hot. But now I need a tissue, or maybe several."

Dev chuckled and leaned to reach the box by the bed. "Here you go."

He took a tissue for himself too, although Ewan had ended up with most of their mess on him.

Ewan grinned. "I guess you can tick frottage off your list, then."

"I think so. It was a lot more fun than I was expecting."

Once they'd mopped up a little, they lay back down together, and Dev tried to ignore all the questions in his head while Ewan held him and kissed him some more.

Was that all part of what he was supposed to be learning? Did the physical affection Ewan showed him after they'd had sex mean something?

Dev wasn't brave enough to ask.

Finally, Ewan pulled away, and he sounded reluctant as he said, "I guess I'd better go. It's getting late."

He got up and started dressing.

Part of Dev wanted to invite him to stay. But it would be so awkward if Ewan said no that he didn't dare risk it. Ewan wasn't his boyfriend, so he probably wouldn't want to sleep in Dev's bed.

Dev sat up and retrieved his own clothes. It was weird being naked around Ewan now they weren't touching anymore.

"How about we get together on Sunday?" Ewan asked. "Text me and let me know what you want to try making."

Dev frowned as he pulled on his T-shirt, confused.

Making what?

Next on the list was fingering. But they wouldn't be doing that till next weekend.

"To eat," Ewan added. "Remember? I'm going to teach you to cook. Find a recipe and send me a link tomorrow. I'll get the ingredients, because I need to go shopping anyway."

"Okay." Dev felt a warm bubble of excitement at the thought of getting to spend more time with Ewan so soon, even if it was to learn cookery rather than sex tips. It was nice to think Ewan was becoming a friend. Dev could use more of those after his unfortunate start to his university life. He hoped that even when his and Ewan's arrangement was over, the friendship might remain.

He stood and pulled his sweatpants back on, then his glasses before following Ewan to the bedroom door.

"You don't need to see me out," Ewan said.

"I want to," Dev insisted.

It was the polite thing to do, plus it gave him a couple of extra minutes in Ewan's company.

Downstairs, Ewan paused at the front door. "You can walk me home if you like." He grinned.

Dev chuckled. "Very funny."

"So, text me about ingredients tomorrow. And I'll see you Sunday."

"Okay."

They stared at each other for an awkward moment, and then Ewan stepped closer and gave Dev a fleeting kiss on the cheek. "Bye, then."

"Bye."

Ewan let himself out, and Dev closed the door behind him with a smile on his face. How could a peck on the cheek set his heart racing almost as fast as Ewan's mouth on his dick?

"Dev, is that you?" Jez's voice called as Dev passed the half-open door to the living room.

"Yeah, what do you want?" Dev walked in.

Jez and Mac were on the sofa where he'd left them earlier, but now Dani was there too, stretched out on the other sofa with her feet up. Jez and Mac had finished gaming. The TV was on instead, showing an old episode of *Friends*.

"Had fun studying, did you?" Dani's voice was teasing, but her expression was kind, not mean.

Dev still tensed and blushed anyway. "Um. Yeah, it was fine."

"It sounded a lot more enjoyable than my usual study sessions." She grinned and Dev's face got even hotter. He tried and failed to come up with an appropriate response, but she saved him. "Stop freaking out, Dev. It's cool. Good for you—Ewan seems nice."

"And now Mac owes me a tenner," Jez said.

"Fuck you, I do not." Mac knocked his knee into Jez's. "I didn't take that bet because I thought they were hooking up too. It was obvious there was something going on, they were looking at each other all gooey-eyed earlier. So, are you guys dating, or what?"

"No!" Dev said quickly. "No, it's not like that. Nothing serious. It's just...." He wasn't sure how to describe it.

"Friends with benefits?" Jez suggested.

"Yeah, I guess."

Jez looked sceptical. "Right. But you want more."

Do I?

Dev wasn't sure what he wanted. "I haven't really thought about it." He squirmed at the lie, because he'd actually thought about it quite a lot, but it hadn't helped him work out his feelings. Anyway, Ewan wasn't looking for a boyfriend. He was only doing Dev a favour. Once the lessons were over, the arrangement would end, so it didn't matter what Dev did or didn't want.

"Well, whatever. I'm glad you're having fun. I think you deserve it after your shitty start to your first year. Things seem to be looking up for you now." Jez smiled at him.

"Yeah." Dev grinned back. He was still embarrassed at Dani having heard him and Ewan through the wall, but his housemates' easy acceptance of his and Ewan's *relationship*—for want of a better word—eased something in his chest. "Yeah, things are definitely looking up."

"You wanna sit down?" Dani tucked her legs up, making space for him.

"Yes, okay." Dev sat and accepted the beer Mac offered him. Even though he didn't like beer much, it was another gesture of friendship and Dev didn't want to turn it down.

As they watched, drank, laughed, and chatted over the TV, Dev got out his phone and pulled up his list of things to do this term. He'd already checked off *Research sex stuff*, *Join Grindr*, and *Get some experience*. Then he checked off *Make some friends* too.

On Saturday, Dev woke late. He'd stayed up past midnight watching TV and chatting to Mac, Jez, and Dani. They were all really nice, he'd decided. He'd been so lucky to end up living here. In the end Dev had drunk three of Mac's beers — they'd tasted better the more he drank — and felt quite tipsy because he didn't normally drink alcohol. When he'd finally gone to bed, he'd slept like a log and was little fuzzy-headed this morning.

Dev reached for his phone and pulled up his reminders. His list looked happily empty, but he had a nagging feeling there was something he was supposed to do. He cast his mind back over the day before, allowing it to linger indulgently on the time he'd spent with Ewan. His morning wood throbbed in response as he recalled their study session yesterday.

Then he remembered. He was seeing Ewan again tomorrow and Ewan was going to teach him how to cook. Unusually, he hadn't added it to his phone at the time Ewan arranged it.

Research recipes, he added to his reminders, plus *Text Ewan*.

Dev started his culinary research after breakfast. He looked up the website his mum had sent him a link to. It had a huge database of recipes, but there was a handy search feature that allowed him to narrow it down by things like how easy the recipe was or how quick it was to prepare. Stir-fries featured a lot in the quick-and-easy section, and

Dev remembered how nice the thing that Mac had made in the wok looked and smelled. So that seemed a good place to start.

He texted Ewan. *Good morning. I was looking at recipes online and thought maybe we could start with a stir-fry?*

Ewan replied a few minutes later. *Good idea. Any particular recipe u fancy trying?*

Dev scrolled through the suggestions on his laptop screen again. There were too many to choose from. *I'm happy for you to choose. You'll know what looks easy.*

Is there anything u don't eat or are allergic to?

No, Dev replied. His dad was a Muslim—albeit a rather lapsed one—and didn't eat pork, but Dev's mum was agnostic and they hadn't encouraged Dev into religion as a child. Dev had no religious beliefs and was happy to eat anything so long as it tasted good.

Okay. I'll pick something and buy the ingredients today.

What time shall I come around tomorrow?

Depends what time you wanna eat. It won't take long to cook, so sixish?

Okay. I'll see you then. Dev was impatient. He wished he was going round there today.

Have a good day, Ewan replied.

You too.

Dev put his phone aside. Over twenty-four hours till he got to see Ewan again, and they were only cooking together tomorrow. Well, he assumed that was all they'd be doing. They hadn't made any arrangement to do anything else, and Friday was their maths-and-sex night. Spending time with Ewan doing something non-sexual sounded good too, and he looked forward to it.

CHAPTER ELEVEN

When he knocked on Ewan's door on Sunday evening, Dev was nervous. He wasn't sure what to expect from the evening, and that put him out of his comfort zone. With their Friday session, Dev knew what was on the cards, maths tutoring followed by whatever Ewan was supposed to teach him. They'd always agreed it in advance.

But tonight felt different. Dev wasn't sure where the boundaries were.

Ewan was his usual friendly self when he let Dev in. "Hi." He gave Dev a kiss on the cheek—a friendly kiss, affectionate but nothing more. It still made butterflies explode in Dev's stomach. "Come in. Are you ready to cook?"

"Yes."

"I hope you're hungry. It looks like the portions are going to be huge." Ewan opened the door to the kitchen, and Dev followed him in.

The room was exactly the same layout as Dev's kitchen next door. They had the same landlord, he guessed, and the houses must have been renovated together. Also like Dev's kitchen, it was busy with other people preparing food. In a house of six people, it was rare to get the kitchen to yourself unless you cooked at unusual hours. Two other blokes were jostling for position at the cooker, one frying bacon, the other heating up something in a pan.

"These guys will be finished soon," Ewan said. "We can start chopping things while we wait, though."

The guys turned at the sound of Ewan's voice. One was tall with wavy brown hair and blue eyes—Ryan, the bloke who'd let Dev in last time he came round. The other guy was shorter and stockier, with sandy ginger hair that was a pale imitation of Ewan's bright red.

"Guys, this is Dev. Dev, Ryan and James."

"Hi," Dev said.

They mumbled greetings, seeming friendly enough, but didn't make any effort to chat. They'd been talking amongst themselves when Dev and Ewan came in, and they went back to their conversation, which appeared to be about the merits of different brands of lager.

"I like the Mexican ones," Ryan was saying. "They definitely taste nicer. Some of the Italian ones are good too."

James shook his head emphatically. "Mate, they all taste the same. Seriously. I challenge you to tell any of them from a supermarket own brand in a blind taste test."

"No way. The more expensive ones *do* taste better."

"They bloody don't."

"They do," Ryan insisted.

Ewan gave Dev a grin. "Ready to do some food prep?"

"Sure, let me wash my hands first."

"Oh, yeah. Good idea. I should probably do that too."

They washed their hands together, taking turns to rinse under the tap.

That done, Ewan started getting ingredients out of the fridge and cupboards. When he got it all assembled, it looked like a lot of food.

"We're making a beef and broccoli stir-fry." Ewan handed a printed recipe to Dev. It looked pretty straightforward. "Here, you start by slicing this onion while I wash the red pepper and peel some garlic and ginger." He gave Dev a chopping board and a dangerous-looking knife.

Dev tried to remember how he'd been taught to chop onions in food tech at school. That was years ago, and he recalled cutting his finger badly in the first minute of the practical part and missing the rest of the lesson because he was sent to the school nurse to be bandaged up.

He cut the onion in half, that seemed like a good way to start.

"Um, Dev, that's not really the best way to do it," Ewan said.

"Oh, sorry."

"It's okay. I shouldn't have assumed. It's easier to chop if you top and tail it first, and then cut it in half lengthways rather than the way you've done it." Ewan took the knife from Dev and demonstrated. "Obviously you've now got four quarters rather than two halves, but see how the layers of the onion work with you if you slice it this way. You end up with nice long slices rather than odd sized chunks. Here, you finish it now."

"Thanks."

Once Dev was done with the onion, Ewan showed him how to chop garlic, grate ginger, deseed the red pepper, and cut that into slices too. By the time they'd broken the broccoli into florets, James and Ryan had finished cooking and taken their food and their argument about beer elsewhere.

"Just the steak to slice now." Ewan slapped the meat onto the chopping board. "We need it in thin strips so it cooks fast. If you halve it lengthways and then slice, that should work."

"How come you know so much about cooking?" Dev asked.

Ewan shrugged. "I always enjoyed it. I like food, so I was interested in making my own. My mum and dad encouraged me. By the time I was fourteen or fifteen, I was cooking for the family a couple of times a week at least." He peered over Dev's shoulder. "That's perfect."

As Ewan put a hand on his hip, Dev jumped and the knife slipped, narrowly missing his fingers. "Shit. That was close."

"Sorry." Ewan's voice was warm, but he squeezed Dev's hip lightly and didn't take his hand away. "I shouldn't distract the chef."

"Aren't you the chef?" The hand *was* distracting Dev. He bit his lip and focused on cutting another careful slice of meat.

"I guess. What does that make you, then?"

"Your bitch?"

Ewan snorted in surprise and amusement. "I was thinking more along the lines of sous chef, or kitchen hand. But my bitch works too." He lowered his voice and added, "I quite enjoy giving you orders."

A frisson of heat rippled through Dev at the husky quality in Ewan's voice. He gripped the knife more tightly. Ewan was right up close behind him now, caging Dev in against the kitchen counter. "I like that too," Dev whispered.

He froze, the cooking forgotten. He wanted to turn around and kiss Ewan, but he wasn't brave enough. Ewan's breath was warm on the back of his neck and Dev's heart thundered in his ears.

The kitchen door opened in a burst of female chatter that cut off abruptly in a surprised "Oh!"

Ewan backed off, leaving Dev breathless and frustrated.

"Hi, Ewan. Who's your friend?"

Dev turned to see a pretty girl with long dark hair and brown skin, flanked by another girl with a brown bob and a sweet smile.

"Dev, this is Nadia and Justine."

"Hello," Dev said.

Nadia — the one with the long dark hair — studied him with interest. Dev felt rather like a specimen under a microscope. "Oh, are you Ewan's study partner?"

Dev looked at Ewan, who answered for him. "Yes, nosy. Dev's the guy who's been helping me with my statistics. He lives next door."

"Oh, of course. That's why I recognise you," Justine said.

"And now Ewan's teaching me to cook," Dev explained. It wasn't a lie, other than by omission, but Nadia still looked rather too knowing. Ewan had probably been a bit too slow to move away when the girls burst in on them. First Dani, and now these two. Secrets were hard to keep in shared houses.

"What are you cooking?" Justine asked.

"Beef stir-fry." Ewan got a wok out of one of the low cupboards.

"Nice."

The girls started clattering around in the kitchen while Dev finished chopping the beef. Nadia put a ready meal in the microwave, and Justine started heating up some soup in a pan.

When Dev had finished, Ewan had the wok on the heat, waiting for him. "We're going to sear the beef first and then take it out so it won't get tough. I've got this on a high heat, so it's going to spit a bit. Watch out."

Dev tipped the meat in, and as predicted it sizzled and splashed hot oil that hit his hands like pinpricks. He pulled them away quickly.

Ewan handed him a slotted spoon. "Just stir it quite often, don't let it stick. Once it's brown all over, we'll take it out again."

The smell of the cooking beef made Dev's mouth water. God, he'd missed good food. He was well and truly fed up of eating out of tins.

When the beef was done and set aside in a bowl, Ewan got Dev stir-frying the onions with the garlic and ginger. Finally they added the other vegetables and carried on frying them.

"Isn't the broccoli going to be a bit crunchy if we don't cook it first?" Dev poked it. The stalks were still very firm and didn't seem to be softening.

"It's not supposed to be too squishy in a stir-fry. But we're going to steam it for a few minutes while we cook the noodles, that will get it just right."

Once the noodles were simmering in a pan, Ewan got Dev to put the meat back in the wok and add the final ingredients: soy sauce, honey, and a dash of water. "Now put the lid on, and the vegetables will cook through a bit."

The scents filling the kitchen were amazing. The rich, meaty smell combined with the ginger, garlic, and soy had Dev's stomach rumbling. "I can't wait to try it. It smells so good."

He smiled at Ewan, who grinned back.

"It does, doesn't it?"

"It smells way better than my boring microwave lasagne," Nadia said wistfully. She had that on a plate along with some salad. "I'm going before I get food envy. Enjoy!" She carried her food out.

Justine poured her soup into a mug, picked up the plate with a sandwich she'd made, and followed Nadia.

Finally they were alone again.

Ewan was leaning against the surface next to the cooker. His arms folded, he was the picture of relaxation. His long body was lean and strong, and Dev's heart spiked as memories of how Ewan's skin felt and smelled pushed into his consciousness. His gaze lingered on the bulge in Ewan's jeans.

The sound of Ewan clearing his throat made Dev start and flush as he snapped his eyes up to see Ewan's amused expression.

Ewan raised his eyebrows and smirked. "Hungry?"

Even Dev couldn't miss the double meaning in the question, but he chose to ignore it. Cheeks burning hotter, he nodded. "Yeah. *Starving*."

The oven timer beeped, breaking the thick tension between them. Dev admired the muscles in Ewan's arms as he stirred the noodles and scooped one out to test. He dangled it off the spoon and bit off the end.

"I think it's done. You try?"

Dev stepped closer, parting his lips obediently. He caught the noodle with his tongue and sucked it into his mouth. He met Ewan's gaze, and the intensity there made heat ripple through him again. Was it normal to feel like that around someone you were having sex with? It was only supposed to be a casual arrangement, but hormones were tricky bastards. Dev hadn't anticipated the inconvenient feelings they caused.

"Don't we need to drain the noodles?" he asked, needing a diversion from Ewan, who was still looking at Dev as though *he* was something edible.

"Oh yeah, shit. And also take the lid off the wok, otherwise we'll end up with soggy noodles *and* soggy broccoli."

Once the noodles were drained, Ewan added them to the wok and Dev stirred till everything combined and the noodles were coated in sauce. Meanwhile, Ewan got out the bowls and cutlery.

When they'd dished up two huge bowls — Ewan was right, the recipe had made very generous portions — they carried their food through to the living room.

The layout was very similar to Dev's house: two sofas, a couple of armchairs, and a large dining table in the bay window.

Ryan and James were on a sofa each, glued to football on the TV, their empty plates abandoned on the coffee table. Ewan and Dev joined Nadia and Justine at the table. They sat opposite each other, and Ewan tucked into his food immediately.

"God, this is great," he said after his first mouthful. "I'm allowed to say that because you did most of the cooking."

Dev took a forkful. It really was good. Ewan wasn't exaggerating. "This is the best thing I've tasted since… I don't know when."

"Since Friday?"

Ewan's tone was innocent, but the words made Dev choke on a mouthful of noodles. He jerked his head up and glared at Ewan, whose grin was anything *but* innocent.

"Need some water?" Ewan pushed Dev's glass towards him.

Dev shook his head and went back to eating. The burn in his cheeks matched the heat in his groin. Hot and bothered from Ewan's teasing, he felt a glow of happiness too. The friendship, the flirting… it was all new and exciting and wonderful. Dev could get used to it.

After they'd eaten, they went back to the kitchen to stack what they could into the dishwasher — only the wok, the pan, the bowls, and the forks needed washing.

"I'll do them," Dev said.

"You don't need to."

"It will only take a minute."

So Dev washed, and Ewan dried and put them away.

"I guess I should go," Dev said, wiping his hands on a tea towel. He didn't want to outstay his welcome. "Thank you for the cooking lesson."

"You're welcome. It was fun. Do you want to do it again this week? Tuesday, maybe, or Wednesday?"

Ewan sounded enthusiastic, and Dev was pretty sure it was a genuine offer. "Yes, I'd love to. Tuesday's good for me."

"Pick another recipe, then, and let me know the ingredients you need."

"Why don't I buy them next time? I was going to give you cash for today, but I could pay for the next lot instead—if that works?"

"Yeah, that sounds good."

Suddenly the tension was back. They stood facing each other, not quite within touching distance, but it wouldn't take much to close the gap.

Ewan licked his lips, and Dev caught the movement, his gaze snagging on the wet pink of Ewan's mouth. Dev wanted to kiss him. Was Ewan thinking about kissing him too?

"I'd better—" Dev said at the same time as Ewan said, "Do you want—?"

The kitchen door burst open again.

"Sorry to interrupt," Nadia said cheerily as she whisked past them to get to the dishwasher. "Don't mind me."

"It's... I'm just leaving anyway." Dev thought he caught a flash of disappointment on Ewan's face, but it was gone before he could be sure.

"I'll see you out," Ewan said.

Ewan not only saw Dev to the front door, he followed him outside into the cool of the evening. His feet were bare and he was only wearing a thin T-shirt.

"What are you doing?" Dev asked.

"Walking you home."

It was about twenty steps from Ewan's front door to Dev's. "Why?"

"Because I want to say goodbye without anyone interrupting us."

"Oh." Dev's heart surged and his knees suddenly felt wobbly. Maybe it was a good thing he had Ewan beside him in case he tripped on the steps.

When they reached Dev's front door. Dev turned to face Ewan again. The street was deserted.

"Alone at last," Ewan said with a smile.

Dev's head was full of questions as Ewan moved forward and put his hands on Dev's shoulders.

What are we doing? Why are we doing this? What does it mean?

But he was loath to ruin the moment by opening his mouth for anything other than Ewan's tongue. Ignoring his racing thoughts, he held his breath and waited.

But the kiss, when it came, was just a soft brush of lips on his cheek and a tantalising scratch of Ewan's stubble. Ewan pulled away before Dev had time to think about how to prolong it or turn it into something more than a friendly peck.

"Good night, Dev."

Dismissed, Dev wilted and tried to hide his disappointment. "Night."

CHAPTER TWELVE

After Dev went inside, Ewan stared at the closed front door for a moment before turning away.

He was sad the evening was already over. He'd been trying to pluck up the courage to ask Dev whether he wanted to come upstairs when Nadia had interrupted them.

Maybe it was for the best. If Dev had turned him down, it would have made things awkward. Ewan didn't want to believe that Dev only wanted him as a sex tutor or gay mentor or whatever the fuck he was. He was almost sure Dev wanted more too. He could see it in the way Dev looked at him, in his sweet receptiveness to Ewan's touch. But he wasn't sure enough to ask Dev how he felt.

Ewan knew he was getting emotionally involved, and he didn't want to make Dev feel uncomfortable if his feelings weren't reciprocated. He'd promised Dev a no-strings arrangement and didn't want to mess things up by admitting his attachment.

He sighed, standing on the doorstep of his own house, lost in thought. The chill of the stone seeped into his feet, reminding him of his lack of shoes. He pushed the door, sure he'd left it ajar, but it was closed and locked now.

"Bugger," he muttered, ringing on the bell and then banging on the door for good measure.

"Where's the fire?" Ryan asked as he opened the door.

"Sorry, someone shut me out."

"Nadia thought you'd gone next door with your new boyfriend."

"He's not my boyfriend." Ewan didn't mean to snap, but it came out sounding pissy.

Ryan raised placating hands as Ewan pushed past him. "Whatever, dude. You know I don't care."

Ewan let out an exasperated sigh. It wasn't fair to take his frustration out on Ryan. He was a good bloke and a good mate. Ewan turned back to him. "Yeah, I'm sorry. I just…." He shrugged.

"You like him." Ryan was perceptive. He might have been all beer and football on the surface, but there was a depth to him that Ewan appreciated.

"Yeah. But it's complicated, though. So I'm not sure it's gonna work out."

"Isn't it always?" Ryan said. "Relationships, man. I'm not sure they're worth the hassle. But I hope it works out for you anyway." Ryan gave him a gentle bro-punch to the shoulder.

"Thanks. Me too." Ewan gave a half-hearted grin before heading up to his room. "See you later."

Ewan got an email from Dev on Monday evening, with a link to a recipe for chicken and mushroom curry.

How about this? It takes a bit longer to cook than the stir-fry, but it looks nice. If you like the sound of it, I'll buy the ingredients on my way home tomorrow. Let me know what time to come over.

Ewan replied. *Sounds great. Any time after 5 is fine with me.*

Dev turned up at five fifteen exactly.

Ewan knew the time because he'd been trying—and failing—not to watch the clock on the TV. He jumped up as soon as he heard the doorbell. "I'll get it, it's probably for me."

"Ooh, is it your new boyfriend?" Nadia asked from where she was painting her nails at the table.

"I'm just cooking with Dev again."

"Like I said…." She grinned knowingly.

Ewan's housemates hadn't let up on him since Sunday night. They all seemed to think he and Dev were an item, and he couldn't be bothered to even try to explain what he and Dev were to each other. He'd let Nadia assume they were dating; it was easier that way.

Dev stood on the doorstep with a wide smile and two carrier bags.

"Come in."

Ewan greeted him with a kiss on the cheek; only after he'd done it, he realised he might be overstepping. But Dev seemed okay with it because his smile widened.

Ewan reached out a hand. "Here let me take one of those."

They carried the bags into the kitchen, which was empty for once, and unpacked the contents. Chicken thighs, onions, mushrooms, a bunch of coriander, a tin of chickpeas, a jar of curry paste, and a can of coconut milk.

"Maybe I should have got the real spices, but the recipe said this brand of curry paste is pretty good," Dev said.

"And it's a lot less stuff to buy."

"Exactly."

"Did you print the recipe off?" Ewan asked.

Dev's face fell. "Oh no. I forgot. Sorry."

"That's okay. I'll run upstairs and do it now. Why don't you start by chopping the onion—remember how I showed you?"

"Sure."

"Okay, back in a sec."

When Ewan returned with the recipe, Dev had chopped the onion—into perfect, even-sized pieces—and was busy washing the mushrooms.

"Nice work." Ewan was impressed. "You're a fast learner."

Dev shot him a glance, cheeks pinking under the bright overhead light. "You already knew that."

Ewan laughed, blushing himself at being caught out in an accidental double-meaning. "I honestly wasn't thinking about that. But yes, I did know. And *now* I'm thinking about it."

Dev grinned and went back to his mushrooms. "Me too."

"Stop distracting me. We've got food to cook."

They worked together seamlessly. Dev followed all Ewan's instructions with impressive attention to detail. Ewan let him do most of the work—he was supposed to be learning, after all—but he kept a close eye on him, standing behind Dev, watching over his shoulder as he chopped and sliced things in the preparation stage.

Once Dev was ready to start cooking, Ewan let Dev get on with it. Dev had the recipe to follow, but Ewan stayed close and answered any questions Dev had. Dev wanted to know details the recipe didn't give.

"How often should I stir the onions? And how high should the gas ring be on?"

"It depends. If you have the heat on higher, you need to stir more often so they don't burn. But on a lower heat you can get away with leaving them for a few minutes at a time."

Dev frowned. "Then how am I supposed to know what to do?"

"Cooking isn't an exact science." Ewan reached around Dev for the wooden spoon to give the onions a poke. "It's more of an art form. You can follow a recipe, sure. But there are some things you need to use your instincts for. You'll get the hang of it with practice—like anything else." He let go of the spoon and put his hand on Dev's hip.

"Practice makes perfect?" Dev's voice was a little husky.

"Yeah." Ewan squeezed Dev's hip and then released him.

Miraculously they were still alone in the kitchen when the curry was finally simmering in a large pan on a low heat.

Dev consulted the recipe. "So now we leave it for twenty minutes."

"Yep." Ewan decided to be bold. It usually worked for him. He stepped forward and took the piece of paper out of Dev's hand, caught his gaze, and held it, quirking an eyebrow. "I had an idea for what we could do while we wait."

Dev licked his lips nervously. "Yeah?"

"I know it's not Friday… but I thought you might want to sneak in an extra practice session, seeing as we've got time to kill."

"Practice at what?" Dev frowned.

Was Dev really that oblivious, or was he playing along? It was hard to tell, sometimes. Ewan decided to go with the direct approach. "Hand jobs? Cocksucking? I'm down for either, or a combination of the two. Or just more kissing if you prefer."

Dev blinked and parted his lips. A sweet flush of embarrassment—or maybe arousal—swept up his neck to his cheeks. "Yeah," he said roughly. "Any... *all* of that sounds good. But have we got time?"

"We can make time. With a recipe like this, the timing is flexible. If it takes us twenty-five minutes instead of twenty, the dinner'll be fine anyway. But I can come in less than five minutes with the right incentive, so I think we'll be okay."

"One minute twenty-two seconds." Dev's lips quirked in a grin.

"Huh?"

"That's my record. But I was pretty turned on already because I'd been watching porn. But from touching myself to coming—that's how long it took."

Ewan snorted and shook his head. "You timed yourself wanking? Only you, Dev."

Dev shrugged, still flushed but looking rather pleased with himself. "I was interested to know."

"Well, I can't promise to make you come in less than one minute twenty-two, but I can have a bloody good try. Come on." Ewan took Dev's hand and tugged him towards the kitchen door. "Let's go and work up an appetite."

They hurried up the stairs to Ewan's room and arrived breathless. Ewan shut and locked the door behind them, then pushed Dev up against the wall and kissed him.

Dev groaned, responding immediately with his hands on Ewan's hips, pulling him closer. Dev clearly wanted this just as much as Ewan did.

Ewan reached for the hem of Dev's T-shirt and pulled it up, breaking the kiss to mutter, "Off."

Dev helped when the fabric got stuck on the frames of his glasses, wriggling free and putting his glasses aside before helping Ewan get out of his T-shirt too. They kissed some more, all warm skin on warm skin and hands everywhere.

Dev was the first to go for the crotch. He cupped Ewan's dick, stroking him through his jeans, finding the shape of Ewan's shaft with clever fingers and rubbing at the head until Ewan moaned, arching into his touch.

"I want to suck you again." Dev murmured, his lips grazing Ewan's cheek.

"God, yes please." Where had the shy, uncertain boy from their first encounters gone?

Dev was already undoing Ewan's buttons, and Ewan went for Dev's trousers, doing the same. They stumbled towards the bed, shoving clothes off awkwardly. Dev almost tripped on his trouser legs, but Ewan held up him. Finally they collapsed onto Ewan's bed in an ungainly sprawl and went right back to kissing.

Ewan was on his back, with Dev kneeling over him, and as Dev started to work his way down, kissing and licking and sucking, Ewan had a genius idea.

"I know what we should try. It wasn't on your list, but we should sixty-nine. It's really hot, and it's time efficient." Really, Ewan didn't give a fuck about efficiency; he just wanted the dual deliciousness of Dev in his mouth while Dev wrapped his gorgeous lips around Ewan's dick.

"I like efficient." Dev raised his head to grin at him.

"I knew you would."

"So, how do we...?"

"Turn around, so I can get at you while you suck me. Or we can both lie on our sides if you prefer." That might feel less exposing for a novice. Ewan remembered the first time he'd straddled someone else's face; he'd been pretty self-conscious about what the other guy could see. With them on their sides, Dev's arse wouldn't be quite so on display.

Apparently, Dev had no such qualms because he was already moving. "Like this?"

He knelt astride Ewan's face, his thick cock right where Ewan wanted it, furry balls swinging gently. Above them, the smooth expanse of Dev's taint led back to his tight little hole. Ewan's dick throbbed at the sight.

Ewan captured Dev's balls in his palm and squeezed lightly. "Yeah. Perfect."

And then Dev took Ewan's cock in his mouth, and Ewan's thinking brain went offline.

After that it was all instinct and sensation, a mutual feedback loop of hot wet mouths and muffled grunts and groans. Ewan used one hand to keep Dev's cock angled for easy sucking, and with the other he caressed Dev's balls, rubbing and stroking, loving the way they tightened under his fingertips.

Dev took a leaf out of Ewan's book, doing the same to him, and it felt so fucking good. But Ewan wanted more. He spread his legs, hoping Dev would get the hint, and was rewarded by a tentative stroke over his perineum and Dev's finger pushing back to where Ewan craved to be touched. He moaned in encouragement as Dev skimmed his fingertip over Ewan's hole, so Dev did it again.

Ewan desperately wanted to return the favour, but knowing it was all new to Dev, he thought he'd better check Dev was down for some arse play tonight. So he pulled off to ask, "Can I do that to you too?"

The response was immediate and very certain. "*Yeah.*"

Ewan grinned, sucked his fingers to make them wet, and then took Dev back into his mouth while sliding his fingers back to find Dev's hole.

Dev tensed, clenching at Ewan's first touch, but as Ewan circled his fingers, Dev relaxed with a moan, his hot breath gusting over Ewan's sensitive cock.

Dev was distracted for a moment, panting as Ewan worked him over, but he must have realised he was slacking because he sucked Ewan with renewed enthusiasm. Dev's fingers were dry on Ewan's hole, but it still felt good. Dev didn't try to push inside, but the gentle stimulation on the sensitive skin sent tingles of pleasure to Ewan's cock, driving him closer to orgasm.

Dev started making desperate little sounds around Ewan's cock, and Ewan knew Dev was close too. He sucked harder, jerking Dev with one hand while rubbing his hole with the other. Dev's body tensed, and then he was coming, filling Ewan's mouth as his hole softened, clenching and releasing under Ewan's stroking fingers. Ewan kept up a steady pressure and the tip of one finger slipped in, making Dev gasp and tighten around it. The grasp of those muscles tipped Ewan over the edge, and he came in a blinding rush, with Dev sucking him right through the wave of pleasure and out the other side.

When Ewan came back to reality, Dev had rolled off him and lay on his back, limbs loose and heavy. He didn't look like he was in any state to move, so Ewan switched ends to lie beside him at the bottom of the bed, their bodies aligned again. He pulled Dev close and kissed him, tasting come—his or Dev's, or maybe a cocktail of both.

Cock-tail.

Ewan smiled at the thought.

"We're the wrong way up," Dev said when Ewan broke the kiss to lie with his head on Dev's shoulder.

"Do you care?"

"No." Dev snuggled closer. "It's your pillow with our feet on it, not mine."

"I'm going to lick your arse soon. I don't care about your feet on my pillow."

Dev drew in a sharp breath. Ewan wondered if he'd shocked him. Dev was such an odd mixture of shy and bold.

"Does it feel good?" Dev asked hesitantly.

"What?"

"Rimming. I mean… it always looks hot in porn. But those guys are paid to look like they're enjoying it. I want to try it, but I always thought it might tickle a lot or just feel weird."

It was confession time. With Dev asking him flat out, Ewan wasn't going to lie about it. "Um… I've never actually tried it." He took Dev's hand and linked their fingers together, hands on Dev's chest. "But I want to, with you. Do you want to give it a go on Friday? We could combine it with fingering — they should go well together."

Too late the thought occurred to him that by rushing through the list, he might be buying himself less time with Dev.

"Yes, okay. Rimming and fingering it is."

Dev sounded so matter-of-fact about it, but somehow that only turned Ewan on more. His cock tingled with renewed interest.

Down, boy.

"I guess we should clean up a little and go and check on the curry," Ewan said.

They got up and dressed quickly.

Dev looked at the clock by Ewan's bed. "We've been up here for seventeen minutes, so by the time we get back down to the kitchen, the curry should be ready."

"Perfect timing." Ewan held out his hand for a high five.

With a grin, Dev slapped his palm, but then his face fell. "We should have put the rice on ten minutes ago!"

Ewan shrugged. "It'll be fine. The curry can simmer for another ten minutes."

"You didn't forget the rice, did you? You should have reminded me," Dev said accusingly.

"Nope. I let you forget about the rice and lured you upstairs for sex. Is that a problem?"

Dev laughed. "No, I guess not."

Down in the kitchen, Ryan was stirring their pan. With the lid off, the fragrance of curry spices filled the room. "Damn this looks amazing. What are you guys making?"

"Chicken and mushroom curry," Ewan replied. "Get your greedy hands off it."

"Hey, I was just checking it for you." Ryan replaced the lid and put the spoon down. "You disappeared. I didn't want it to burn while you were off… doing whatever you were doing." The grin on his face suggested his imagination might not have strayed too far from reality.

"It would have been fine. But thanks for your concern."

"You're lucky," Ryan said to Dev. "I've been trying all year to get Ewan to cook for me. What's your secret?"

"Um." Dev seemed at a loss.

"I'm not cooking *for* him, I'm cooking *with* him," Ewan explained. "Dev's a maths genius, and he's helping me with my stats assignments. It's fair exchange. Whereas you don't do anything for me apart from steal my milk and borrow money off me."

"Sad but true," Ryan sighed, mock tragic. "I clearly need to find something you want." He raised his eyebrows at Ewan and gave him a dirty grin.

Sometimes Ryan was really flirty for a straight guy — or straight so far as Ewan was aware.

"Shall I put the water on for the rice?" Dev asked.

Ewan shifted his attention back to the task in hand. "Yes, sure. I'm starving."

Once the rice had cooked, they dished up the curry and went through to the living room to eat. Nadia and Justine were sitting at the dining table with their laptops, books and papers spread out everywhere.

"Oh, sorry. We're in the middle of an essay crisis. Do you need us to move?" Justine asked.

"No, it's fine. We're okay on the sofa." Ewan sat on the sofa with his plate on his lap.

Dev joined him. The TV was off, but music played in the background.

"How is it?" Ewan asked after Dev's first taste.

"Delicious." Dev nodded his approval.

After that they ate in silence, punctuated by the rustling of paper, the tapping of laptop keys, and the drift of occasional conversation from the girls.

Once they'd finished, Dev insisted on washing up again.

The recipe had made enough for four people and quite a lot was left, so Ewan put a portion of curry in a plastic tub for Dev to take away. "That's your dinner for tomorrow sorted."

When it was time for Dev to leave, Ewan saw him out again. Like last time, he gave Dev a chaste kiss on the cheek. He wanted more, but didn't want to blur the lines of their arrangement in case he scared Dev away.

"Goodbye," Ewan said softly. "See you Friday, I guess?"

"Yeah." Dev smiled. "See you Friday."

Ewan sighed as he walked back to his own front door. He was impatient for Friday already, even though it would take them one step closer to the end of Dev's lessons. The thought of this being over made his heart twist. Dev would be hard to give up.

CHAPTER THIRTEEN

Dev had just finished fixing an issue with one of the library computers at the end of his shift on Thursday afternoon, when a familiar voice greeted him.

"Hi Dev, haven't seen you in a while. How's things?"

Dev turned to see Rupert smiling at him in a way that might once have made Dev's heart flutter. Interestingly, he now appeared to be immune. Not that Rupert wasn't handsome — he was still good to look at — but he wasn't having the same effect on Dev that he used to.

"Hey. I'm pretty good, thanks. Great, in fact."

Rupert looked at his watch. "I just finished for the day. Are you done here? Want to go and grab a coffee and catch up?"

"Sure. Let me just test this is working okay." Dev rebooted the computer and ran a few checks. It all looked good.

"Nice work," Rupert said. "Shall we?"

Dev stopped at the front desk to let the librarians know he'd finished, and everything was working properly now.

A mild spring afternoon with a clear blue sky and bright sunshine greeted them outside, so Dev and Rupert went to one of the campus cafés that had outdoor seating.

Situated in a busy area of campus, the café's outside tables were full, but students sat on a grassy area nearby and congregated on walls, benches, and steps. Dev ordered his usual chocolate milkshake while Rupert got a coffee.

"So," Rupert said when they found a free bench outside to sit on. "It's working out well in the new house, then?"

"Yeah. It's great. I'm so grateful to you for helping me find it."

"Shawn's not giving you any trouble?"

"No. I hardly see him, to be honest. He's got a girlfriend and spends a lot of time over at her place. Mike isn't around much either but he seems okay. And Mac, Jez, and Dani are all really nice."

"I'm glad." Rupert studied Dev intently. "You look like a different person."

"How?"

"I don't know, exactly. Just... more relaxed. You had a kind of tense, hunted look about you before, and it's gone. You look happy."

Dev smiled. "I am happy."

Dev hadn't realised it until he said it, but he was truly content. Even before all the horrible shit with Matt and the other guys in his corridor, Dev hadn't been happy. Although he'd wanted to come to uni, leaving home had been stressful. He found change difficult and just as he'd started to feel settled, everything had gone wrong. Now, at last, he was living somewhere he could relax, with people who liked him for who he was. "My new housemates are cool, and I've also made friends with this guy who lives next door."

Dev's smile widened. Ewan was one of the best things about his life at the moment. Even thinking about him made Dev feel all warm and gooey inside, like melted chocolate, or marshmallow.

"Dev?" Rupert snapped his fingers in front of Dev's face, and Dev realised he'd been staring into space with a goofy grin.

"Sorry," he said.

"I lost you there for a minute." Rupert's expression was amused. "This guy next door must be really something."

Just then, as though conjured up by Dev's imagination, he caught sight of a familiar figure walking along. Ewan's head was angled down towards his phone; he was going to pass them without noticing.

"Ewan!" Dev called out before he could think better of it.

Ewan's head snapped up at the sound of Dev's voice, and he greeted him with a huge smile as he crossed the space between them.

Ewan stopped in front of them. "Hi." His gaze drifted uncertainly to Rupert, and his smile dimmed a little.

"Hi, Ewan." Dev's stupid grin seemed stuck to his face, and he couldn't shake it. "Um" — he gestured to Rupert — "this is Rupert, a friend of mine. The one who helped me move, remember? Rupert, this is Ewan, my... one of my new neighbours."

"Ah." Rupert shot Dev a knowing glance.

Ewan nodded and stuck out a hand to Rupert. "Hi. You're the guy who helped Dev find the room?"

"Yeah. Hi, Ewan." Rupert shook Ewan's proffered hand.

Ewan still looked a little wary, and Dev wasn't sure why.

"Why don't you join us?" Rupert asked. He moved away from Dev to make space for Ewan between them.

Ewan sat. "What are you guys up to?"

"Just catching up. I haven't seen Dev since he moved in," Rupert said.

"So, how did you know about the room in the house, then?" Ewan asked. "What's the connection?"

"I know Jez and Mac. My boyfriend, Josh, used to live with them before he moved in with me a few months ago."

"Oh, that's cool." Ewan relaxed then, the tension leaving his posture as he settled against the back of the bench.

"Josh was asking about you the other day, actually, Dev," Rupert said. "I'd been meaning to text. Hey — you should come over for dinner sometime. How about tomorrow night. Are you free?"

"No. I'm… we're…." He glanced at Ewan. "I'm studying with Ewan tomorrow."

"Saturday, then?" Rupert persisted. "Why don't you come too, Ewan? You'd be very welcome."

"Okay, I can do Saturday." Dev's stomach turned over at the casual way Rupert extended the invitation to Ewan.

"Me too, thanks."

Ewan sounded happy with the arrangement, but Dev felt flustered. He wasn't sure what assumptions Rupert had made about them.

Rupert finished his coffee. "I'd better get going. It was great to meet you, Ewan, and I'll see you both on Saturday — about seven?"

"Okay."

Rupert stood, and Dev got up too. Rupert gave him a hug goodbye. "See you!"

Dev sat back down next to Ewan as Rupert strode off.

"He seems nice," Ewan said.

"Yeah. He's a good guy." Dev offered his cup to Ewan. It was still half-full. "Here, do you want some of my milkshake?"

"Thanks." Ewan took it with a grin.

They finished it, passing it back and forth between them. When they'd emptied the glass, Ewan asked, "Are you heading home now?"

"Yeah."

"Me too."

They walked through the city streets together. Dev hesitated at the steps that led to his front door. He wished he was brave enough to ask Ewan in, but for what? He didn't have anything interesting to cook tonight, and they already had an arrangement for Friday. They'd broken their routine once this week, but that had been Ewan's idea, and Dev didn't know how to ask for what he wanted. "I'll see you tomorrow, then?" he said instead.

"Yeah." Ewan stepped close and kissed Dev on the cheek as he always did. It was sweet and lingered a little, but it wasn't enough, and Dev wanted so much more. "See you tomorrow."

Dev went up to his room and threw himself onto his bed in frustration.

He's not your boyfriend, he told himself firmly. *That's not what this is.*

He remembered Ewan talking about how he liked to be young, free, and single. Maybe that was what Dev needed to be for a while. Once finished with the arrangement with Ewan, hopefully he'd have the confidence to date or hook up. He would need to do something, or he'd be right back to square one: forever alone. He got out his phone and pulled up his long-term list of things to do. Looking over the items he'd checked off, he reassured himself he was still on track, working on the cooking and getting some experience. Once he was done with those things, the only item left was *Find a boyfriend*.

Dev found it even harder than usual to concentrate on explaining things to Ewan on Friday. With the promise of rimming and fingering in his future, he was practically squirming on his chair as he imagined what they would be doing as soon as they were done with the chapter on chi-squared tests.

In preparation for tonight, Dev had done some research and ordered a douche online to make sure he was squeaky clean inside as well as out. Thankfully the delivery guy had brought it to the right house this time, and Dev had been there to answer the door. Imagining somebody else opening *that* by mistake, Dev felt hot all over.

He'd used the douche earlier, along with a very thorough shower, but nerves and anticipation were making him sweat. The sooner they got naked the better.

It seemed like forever before Ewan finally finished the last problem Dev had set him. Was he working more slowly than usual tonight, or was Dev simply more impatient?

"Okay, I'm done." Ewan pushed his paper towards Dev. "Do you want to check it?"

Dev snatched it out of his hand and studied the figures carefully, running his fingertip down the page as he went. "It's fine." His hand shook a little as he put the page down on the desk. He took a steadying breath.

"You look nervous," Ewan said.

Dev met Ewan's gaze. The light from the desk lamp made his irises almost golden, but his pupils were large pools you could get lost in.

"Nervous, excited, tense," Dev admitted. Ewan put his hand on Dev's thigh, and Dev realised only then that he was jiggling his leg up and down. He forced himself to stop, letting out an apologetic huff of laughter. "Sorry. I'm pretty keyed up."

Ewan stood and offered him a hand. "Come on, let's just get on with it. It's like anything else. You won't be nervous once you get started."

He led Dev over to the bed and they lay down together. Ewan distracted him with kisses until Dev's nerves fled, replaced by arousal and hunger for more of Ewan's touch.

Dev was the one to take things further, shedding his T-shirt and removing Ewan's to get at his skin. They took a break from snogging to get naked, and Dev went to lock the door.

When he came back to the bed, Ewan had stretched out on his back and was eyeing Dev's erection and stroking his own. "What do you want to try?"

Dev's heart fluttered as he lay down beside Ewan again. He knew what he wanted, but it was really hard to say the words. "I, um, want to try what we talked about." He hoped Ewan had a good memory.

"Rimming?"

Dev nodded.

"But who gets to go first? Or we could try sixty-nine again?"

"I think I'd rather take turns." Dev had read up on rimming techniques but he didn't trust his ability to put theory into practice while Ewan was licking him at the same time.

"Toss you for it?" Ewan smirked, fisting his dick suggestively.

Dev chuckled. "I think that would rather defeat the purpose." Feeling brave, he said decisively, "I'll do you first. Turn over." That seemed like the lesser of two — not evils exactly, but awkwardnesses. The thought of being face down with his arse in the air for Ewan made Dev hot all over, and not entirely in a good way. He'd rather be giving first instead of receiving.

Perhaps Ewan felt the same because when he rolled onto his front, he hid his face in his arms. "Like this?"

Dev knelt astride one of Ewan's thighs. "You'll need to spread your legs a little wider, and maybe tilt your hips up a bit."

Ewan obliged, and Dev's cock jerked at the first sight of Ewan's hole: tight and pink in Ewan's lightly furred crease, oddly inviting, yet intimidating at the same time. Dev hoped Ewan had showered that evening. Dev didn't think he could ask, but surely Ewan would have done so when he knew *this* was on the cards?

"Dev?" Ewan's voice was muffled. "I'm ready when you are."

"Oh, sorry." Dev realised he was starting at Ewan's arse like an idiot, and that probably wasn't doing much for Ewan's confidence. Ewan was as inexperienced with this side of things as Dev was. He must be nervous too.

He put his hands on Ewan's buttocks. Starting slowly seemed like a good idea, so he stroked them, enjoying the raspy tingle of hair against his palms. Ewan tensed and then relaxed, settling more comfortably on the bed as Dev massaged him for a few moments.

Dev lowered himself so he could use his mouth as well as his hands. He kissed the taut globes of Ewan's arse cheeks, first one side and then the other, then back to the first. As he kissed back and forth, he gradually worked his way closer to Ewan's cleft.

"Tease," Ewan muttered. But it didn't sound like a complaint. He tilted his hips up in invitation.

Dev dropped lower to kiss the skin behind Ewan's balls. That elicited a gasp, so he did it again with more enthusiasm, licking and sucking as he inched his way higher. Ewan smelled of shower gel and clean sweat, but beneath those layers was a musky earthiness that was new and exciting to Dev, subtly different to the scent he remembered in Ewan's groin.

Feeling brave, Dev used his hands to push Ewan's buttocks apart and gain access. He licked a stripe right up Ewan's crack, feeling the texture of the skin change under his tongue.

Ewan let out a grunt, tensing as Dev's tongue passed over his hole. "Fuck."

Dev was pretty sure it was a sound of approval, so he did it again.

"Fuck. Yeah."

Definitely approval, then. Dev grinned and carried on. He focused his attention on Ewan's hole now, circling and pressing until he felt the muscle soften.

Ewan made a hoarse sound and spread his legs wider, pushing back against Dev's mouth. Dev licked harder, deeper, tasting sweat and something almost metallic. He carried on, focused on Ewan and the noises he was making. Ewan seemed to be really into it. But after a while, Dev's jaw started to ache and he didn't think Ewan was going to come like this.

He pulled away and studied Ewan's hole. The skin was even pinker now, and it was wet and shiny with Dev's spit. "Was that good?" he asked Ewan. "Sorry, I had to stop. My jaw got tired."

Ewan chuckled. "Yeah. I can imagine. And yeah, it felt really good. Now I know what all the fuss is about. Do you want to try it?"

"Yeah." Dev really did. Especially after seeing Ewan's reaction.

"Swap places, then." Ewan rolled to the side, and Dev took his spot.

Dev's cock had softened while he was concentrating on Ewan, but as he lay face down and spread his legs for Ewan, a pulse of arousal beat through him making his cock thicken with anticipation.

"It feels so…." Dev couldn't think of the right word. *Slutty* was wrong because sex was normal and natural. "I feel so vulnerable like this. So exposed."

"You are." Ewan pressed a kiss to the small of Dev's back. "But I'll take care of you."

Dev knew he would. He wasn't always the best judge of character, but he trusted Ewan deep in his bones. Ewan was a good guy, a friend. Dev was safe with him. He settled on the bed, forcing himself to relax, and closed his eyes.

"You've got a seriously nice arse," Ewan said admiringly. He ran his hands up Dev's thighs and then teasingly back down. He did this a few times, skimming higher with each movement until finally he gripped Dev's buttocks and squeezed.

Dev tensed, waiting. His cock was rock hard again, and as he shifted his hips, the tip rubbed deliciously on the duvet beneath him. He felt the warm huff of Ewan's breath on his balls.

"Ewan." Dev's voice came out tight and desperate, but he was past caring.

"Mmm?"

The sound was a vibration against Dev's taint as Ewan pressed his lips to the sensitive skin in one kiss, then another, then another, gradually creeping closer to where Dev craved him. "You're such a bloody *tease*," Dev huffed.

"Yep." Ewan chuckled.

Dev was wound so tight that the first touch of Ewan's tongue nearly sent him into orbit. The warm, wet flicker against his hole was simultaneously so good and so porntastically dirty that Dev gripped the pillow his face was pressed into and moaned.

"Is that good?" Ewan paused for just a second to ask the question before licking Dev again.

"Yeah," Dev gasped, hardly able to manage a coherent answer. He bit his lips, trying to stop himself from making more embarrassing sounds. But then he remembered how Ewan had sounded while Dev did this to him, and how much he'd enjoyed Ewan's enthusiastic responses. It was only fair to let Ewan know how good this was. It was almost impossible to keep silent, anyway, with Ewan's tongue sliding hotly over Dev's sensitive skin, setting his nerve endings alight with pleasure.

It was so good, but after a while it wasn't enough. Dev wanted — needed more. Too desperate to be self-conscious anymore, he lifted his hips, pushing back against Ewan's flickering tongue and moaning. He was rewarded by the firmer pressure of a finger circling his hole and Ewan's breath skimmed the small of Dev's back as he said, "You ready for this now?"

"Yes," Dev said, breathless and needy.

Ewan teased his hole for a few moments more, dipping in and making Dev clench around him, but not giving him what he really wanted. Dev made a noise somewhere between a whine and a whimper, and Ewan chuckled. "You really want my fingers, huh?"

Dev didn't bother to answer. He assumed it was obvious enough from the way he pushed back again and groaned in frustration.

"Okay. Let me get the lube."

Dev was wound as tight as a spring. Every sound in the room was part of the torture. The too-slow slide of the drawer by his bed, the snick of the bottle cap, the rustle of the bedclothes as Ewan moved in behind him again, one hand firm on Dev's hip.

"Lift up a little," Ewan ordered.

Dev lifted. The new position left him even more vulnerable with his arse on display and his aching cock hanging heavy beneath him. He closed his eyes and let his head drop. He wanted this so much.

Ewan's fingers were back, pressing more insistently now, and Dev's body opened eagerly, accepting them, taking them.

It was Ewan who groaned now. "Fuck, Dev. You feel so good inside."

Dev gripped the covers, trying to bite back a grunt of protest as Ewan pushed them in deep. Deeper than Dev could manage himself. He'd fucked himself on his dildo before, he knew he could take it as long as he relaxed, but having someone else in charge was different.

"Is that too much?" Ewan asked and stopped with his fingers buried inside Dev and one firm hand on Dev's hip.

"No it's... just go slow."

"Of course. Sorry."

Ewan kept his fingers still, allowing Dev to adjust while he smoothed his other hand up and down Dev's back, stroking him with gentle touches that distracted him from the burn in his arse.

Dev deliberately squeezed Ewan's fingers with his muscles, and then focused on relaxing as he exhaled in a long slow huff. "Okay," he said.

Ewan started to move again, a barely perceptible shift at first. Dev felt exposed and raw... but then Ewan's fingers brushed his prostate with a just-right stroke and all Dev's misgivings burned away in a bolt of white-hot pleasure. He made an incoherent sound of approval.

"Yeah?" Ewan's voice sounded as if he was smiling.

"Yeah," Dev managed.

Ewan kept fingering him in slow careful strokes that got Dev perilously close to coming, even without a hand on his cock. Giving himself up, letting someone else touch him so intimately and take control of his pleasure was intense. Dev was making sounds, desperate sounds he'd be embarrassed about if he wasn't so turned on.

"God, Dev. You're so fucking hot. Do you think you can come like this?" Ewan asked, his voice hoarse.

He sounded almost as desperate as Dev felt. "I don't know… maybe? I've done that with my dildo a couple of times, but I usually jerk off as well because I get impatient."

"Jesus," Ewan muttered, still fucking Dev with his fingers.

"What?"

"Just imagining it. Fuck, Dev. I want to see you do that."

"I could show you." With the mind-melting sensation of Ewan's fingers stroking his prostate, there wasn't much Dev wouldn't agree to do for Ewan at that moment.

Dev hadn't realised Ewan meant right then. It wasn't until Ewan carefully withdrew his fingers, making Dev gasp at the loss, that he grasped Ewan's intention.

"Where is it?" Ewan asked.

"In a box under my bed." Dev twisted around to look at Ewan. His face was flushed and his pupils blown wide. "It's got a combination lock."

Dev rolled onto his back and bit his lip while Ewan got the box. Dev's mind was racing.

Am I really going to do this? Do I want to?

His body cried out for it. His arse was empty without Ewan's fingers, and the dildo would feel even better. Fingers were good because they belonged to someone else, but they were kind of bony and had unpredictable fingernail edges. The soft give of the toy was more forgiving and would be easier to fuck himself with—or to be fucked with.

The dirty grin on Ewan's face as he put the box beside Dev was the deciding factor. That and Ewan's rock-hard dick, which made Dev wonder how it would feel to get fucked by *that* instead of by a silicone one.

Next time.

"What's the code?" Ewan asked.

Dev hesitated for just a fraction of a second before replying. "Zero six nine."

Ewan snorted. "How original for a sex-toy storage box. Nobody would ever crack that, Dev." He opened the box and lifted out the blue dildo, stroking it admiringly. "It really is a beauty."

"Give it to me, then," Dev said.

"Yeah baby, I love it when you talk dirty. You want this dick in your arse?" Ewan slapped his palm with the dildo and squeezed the shaft.

Dev glared at him.

"Okay, okay." Ewan handed it over and offered Dev the lube too. Then he settled himself between Dev's thighs, kneeling and stroking his own cock lazily as Dev lubed up the dildo.

Dev spread his legs wider and drew his knees up. Ewan fixed his gaze on Dev's arse and licked his lips. Dev shivered, remembering how Ewan's tongue had felt on him.

The dildo slid in easily, filling the space where Ewan's fingers had been. Dev arched and moaned at the perfect stretch of it, the delicious fullness as it pressed against his prostate.

"Yeah," Ewan murmured, stroking his cock with one hand and Dev's thigh with the other. "Fuck yourself. I wanna see."

Ewan's eyes were intent, his face flushed, and Dev was so turned on by the whole situation. Doing it with Ewan watching heightened every sensation. He wondered how he must look, and his whole body prickled with heat as he imagined what Ewan was seeing. The subtle edge of shame only sent another flash of arousal through him.

"You look so hot," Ewan said, nothing but blatant appreciation in his voice.

Ewan wasn't judging Dev for doing it. He wanted it too. Dev was only giving him what he'd asked for. That gave Dev the confidence to follow Ewan's instructions. He moved the dildo slowly in and out, groaning at the sensation, his cock aching and leaking on his belly with each thrust. It was so good, so right. With Ewan kneeling over him muttering words of encouragement, Dev almost felt like Ewan was fucking him.

"Yeah, that's it. Take that cock," Ewan's eyes were glassy, his hand moving rapidly on his dick. "So fucking sexy. Look at you."

Dev groaned, working the dildo faster, harder. Even with the handle, it was awkward doing it to himself. Arousal made him bold. "You do it. I want you to do it for me."

"Okay." Ewan grabbed Dev's hips and hauled him closer, so Dev's thighs were draped over Ewan's where he knelt. He took the handle of the dildo from Dev's sweaty hand and started to work it. "Like that?"

"Yeah… nearly, a little more like…." Dev put his hand over Ewan's and guided him, changing the angle slightly and gasping as he hit the spot. "Oh God, yes. There."

Ewan curled his free hand around Dev's cock. "You want this too? Are you going to come for me?"

Dev's only answer was a moan as the dual sensations of Ewan's hand on his dick and the dildo in his arse robbed him of the ability to speak. Thankfully, Ewan seemed to realise everything was good, because he carried on, moving his hands in sync and rocking Dev's world. Everything narrowed down to the overwhelming urge to come, coiling tight in Dev's pelvis and flowing out in a burst of relief as he finally clenched tight around the dildo. He arched off the bed and his cock pumped come into Ewan's fist. Dev cried out, unable to even try to stifle the sound as pleasure tore through him, leaving him weak and panting as the wave of ecstasy passed.

Dimly aware of the loss of Ewan's hands, he opened his eyes to see Ewan jerking himself off, his jaw slack as he stared at Dev like a starving man eyeing a three-course meal. His gaze moved from Dev's arse where the dildo still filled him, to Dev's cock, to the come on his stomach. The muscles in Ewan's arm bulged as he stroked himself, and when he finally came with a cry to match Dev's, his whole body shook with it, abs tensing and releasing as he shot all over Dev.

"Oh my God." Ewan collapsed on his back beside Dev, throwing one arm over his face.

Dev eased the dildo out. He had to sit up and reach over the still-motionless Ewan for the tissues.

"You okay?" Dev asked after he'd cleaned up a little. He wondered whether he should have helped Ewan finish or offered to suck him off.

"Fuck yes. Or I will be when I come back to earth. That was so hot."

"Are you sure?"

Ewan uncovered his face and looked incredulously at Dev. "Totally sure. Did you *see* how hard I just came? Watching you drove me crazy. Better than any porn I ever saw."

Dev grinned, a warm, satisfied feeling crept through him. "Awesome."

"Come here." Ewan pulled Dev back down and rolled onto his side to kiss him. "You aced it again," he said. "A plus."

The reminder that this was part of their skill exchange and not a real relationship made the smile fade from Dev's face. "I didn't really do much today. It was mostly you."

"You rimmed me like a pro." Ewan kissed him again, his hand on Dev's face, fingers skimming his jawline.

It was hard to remember Ewan wasn't his boyfriend when he touched Dev like that after sex. Ewan was so affectionate, his touch more loving than sensual. Dev kissed him back; it was easier than talking about it.

"You don't really need me. I think you're a natural," Ewan added when they broke apart again.

But I like you.

Dev wanted to say it, but his courage failed him before he could form the words. "Thanks," he said lamely instead.

They lay tangled for a while. They gave up on talking and focused on kissing and touching. When they cooled down, they pulled the covers up and carried on. Both of them got hard again, but neither made any move to take things further.

Dev enjoyed the easy intimacy, the sweetness of it. He didn't want the evening to end, and Ewan appeared equally reluctant.

When Dev couldn't keep in a yawn, Ewan finally pulled away. "I'd better go."

Dev wanted to ask him to stay. But he didn't. Instead he nodded and got out of the bed to pull on some sweatpants and a T-shirt. When he turned around, Ewan was dressed too.

"So," Ewan said, "I'll see you tomorrow, then."

"If you're sure you want to come? You don't have to." Dev didn't want Ewan to feel obliged. Ewan didn't know Josh and he'd barely met Rupert. Why would he want to give up a Saturday night to hang out with Dev and his friends?

Something like hurt flashed over Ewan's features but was gone before Dev could be sure. "Why wouldn't I want to come? I get free dinner out of it, don't I? It'll make a change not having to cook for myself." He smiled, but there was still a hint of uncertainty there. "Dev. Are you okay with me coming? If you'd rather go on your own, just say."

"No. No it's fine." Dev felt hot and awkward. He wished he'd never started the conversation. He'd made Ewan feel unwelcome, and that was never his intention. "It will be nice to have you there."

"Okay, so call for me tomorrow. Can we walk there?"

"Yeah it's about twenty minutes away. So I'll come by around quarter to seven."

"Cool." Ewan's smile was relaxed again.

"I'll see you out."

Dev followed Ewan down the stairs. They passed Shawn on the middle landing on his way to the bathroom. Dev gave him a nervous smile.

Shawn nodded at him, then looked suspiciously at Ewan. "Alright," he muttered in greeting.

Dev breathed out a sigh of relief.

"Hi," Ewan said breezily.

When they reached the ground floor, Ewan turned and muttered quietly. "He's a ray of sunshine, isn't he?"

"He's an idiot." Dev rolled his eyes. "But a harmless one." He realised as he said it that it was true. Shawn might be a bit of a twat, but Dev didn't see him as a threat. Not like the guys he'd lived with before.

On the doorstep, he gave Ewan a hug and a brief kiss goodbye, and he didn't care that someone might see them. It was a good feeling.

CHAPTER FOURTEEN

Ewan went to a lot of trouble deciding what to wear for dinner on Saturday. He didn't want to appear as if he'd made too much effort, but he wanted to look good. Even though they weren't a couple, he wanted Dev to be proud to be seen with him. After trying on several combinations, he settled on a long-sleeved greyish-blue henley that emphasised his broad shoulders and lean torso, and his favourite pair of jeans because they made his arse look nice.

He studied himself in his mirror and ran his fingers through his artfully tousled red hair. Ewan had hated it when he was younger. Even in Scotland, where there were more ginger genes than average, he'd still been teased for his flaming hair and freckles. Ewan had longed for dark hair and skin that tanned, features he found attractive on other boys. But he'd grown used to his looks, and now he liked what he saw when he stared at his reflection. He hoped Dev would like it too.

Ewan's phone buzzed in his pocket and he pulled it out to see Dev's message on his screen.

Sorry, I'm running a little late. I'll be round in ten minutes.

Ewan checked the time and saw it was six forty, so Dev was only going to be five minutes late. Ewan didn't think he knew anyone else who would bother to apologise for that. He smiled.

No worries, he replied.

Exactly ten minutes later, Ewan was waiting in the living room when the doorbell rang. "That'll be Dev." He got up before anyone else could.

"Hot date?" Ryan asked, his mouth full of cold pizza.

"Something like that." Ewan ignored Ryan's wolf whistle as he left the room.

His heart did a little flip at the sight of Dev on the doorstep. It was a gorgeous evening, the sun was low in the deep blue sky, and it cast Dev in a golden light.

Dev smiled at Ewan, and Ewan grinned back goofily.

"Hi," Dev said.

"Hey." Ewan stepped forward and gave Dev a quick kiss on the cheek. He wanted to kiss him on the lips, but he stopped himself. They only kissed on the lips during sex—or in the aftermath—and Ewan was afraid to cross the invisible line between them.

Walking down their road together, for Ewan it was as if they were on a date. It would have been so natural to reach for Dev's hand and thread their fingers together, or to put an arm around him. On the residential streets around the university, mostly populated by students, Ewan didn't feel the need to hide. If he and Dev were boyfriends, Ewan would want the world to know.

"I wanted to stop and buy something to take— wine, or beer maybe?" Dev asked when they reached the busier road with shops and pubs on it.

"Oh yeah. Good idea."

They went into the little supermarket and studied the impressive array of alcohol. For a small shop, it gave up a lot of shelf space to booze, mostly at the cheaper end of the price spectrum. The manager obviously knew their market and catered for students.

"What do you think I should get?" Dev asked.

"Whatever you like drinking, I suppose. They'll probably open it. Do you prefer beer or wine?"

Dev shrugged. "I don't usually drink either. Beer's too bitter."

"Cider, then, or a sweeter wine? Or we could take some soft drinks too."

"Wine seems appropriate." Dev grinned. "It feels very grown-up to be going to someone's house for dinner."

"We are grown up."

"Obviously. I don't feel it, though. When do you think people start to feel like adults?"

Ewan shrugged. "I dunno. My mum says she still feels eighteen on the inside. So maybe never."

They chose a bottle of red wine. Neither of them had a clue whether it was any good or not, but it came from the top shelf and cost twice as much as the cheapest one. Hopefully that meant it was okay.

They queued, and Dev paid, but Ewan gave him some cash for his half.

"You don't need to," Dev protested.

"Take it. We're holding up the queue."

Back outside, the breeze was fresh. Ewan zipped up his jacket as they walked. Their route led them through the centre of town and up over the Hoe towards the sea. It was exposed up in Hoe Park, the wind whipping their hair and chilling Ewan's ears and fingers even though it was May. He turned up the collar of his jacket.

"Here." Dev took off his beanie and offered it to Ewan.

"Thanks." Ewan pulled it gratefully over his ears.

Dev pulled his hood up and then laughed as the wind blew into his face and pushed it straight back down. He tried again, tying the drawstring until just his face peeked out.

Ewan nudged him. "You look ridiculous."

"I don't care." Dev's smile was brilliant and his cheeks were pink from the wind.

The wind didn't let up as they descended on one of the many paths that led down to the road curving along the seafront.

Dev paused for a moment. "I want to look at the view."

Ewan stopped beside him. "It's beautiful."

"Isn't it? I always wanted to live by the sea. I love everything about it. The smell, the sound, the way the colour changes depending on the sky."

The sea was a deep blue-grey, choppy from the stiff breeze. As the sun dipped lower, the water would darken, highlighted by the contrasting hues of the sunset. Ewan wished they could stay and watch the sun sink below the horizon, although the expression on Dev's face as he gazed out over the water was even more compelling than the view. Lost in childlike wonder, Dev stared, a smile of pure contentment turning up the corner of his lips.

Something tugged at Ewan's heart. "We're gonna be late for your friends." His voice came out with a rough edge.

Dev checked the time on his phone. "Yeah, okay. Sorry." They started walking again, and Dev added, "I always get a little carried away by the sea. Growing up in Oxford, the sea was always this mysterious delight I associated with holidays and rare weekend trips. Living here, I can see it every day if I want, but it's still a novelty."

They descended the steps to the road and followed it along the seafront towards the new developments that stood between the older terraced houses and the water.

"Rupert's flat's in the building at the far end." Dev pointed to a swanky new build with huge windows and balconies.

"Wow, it looks nice." Ewan was impressed.

"Yeah. It's really cool."

"You've been here before, then?"

"Only once. I don't know Rupert all that well," Dev admitted. "We work together. I do some part-time IT support at the uni, and he's my manager. He was always nice to me, but then when everything went wrong with the guys in my corridor, I was still upset the day after at work. Rupert noticed. He took me back to his place that evening. He and Josh were awesome. They made me dinner and got me to tell them everything, and then he helped me find the place I live in now."

They reached Rupert's doorstep. Dev located the bell — one of the top ones — and pressed it.

A tinny voice came through the intercom. "Hi, is that you, Dev?" It didn't sound like Rupert; Rupert had a posher accent.

"Yes."

"Come on up."

The door buzzed, allowing them access.

"They're on the top floor. Do you want to get the lift?" Dev asked.

"Might as well. Looks a long way up."

Ewan's stomach swooped as the lift rose. He wasn't sure if it was gravity or nerves about the evening. The whole thing was weirdly date-like, yet not. He wanted to make a good impression on Dev's friends even though he told himself it didn't really matter.

The guy who greeted them at the door of the flat was cute. His floppy dark hair fell into his eyes, and he swept it aside as he beamed at them. Slim built like Dev, he was a little shorter, but he moved with grace and confidence that was very *un*like Dev, who tended towards the clumsy.

"Dev, hi." He pulled Dev into an affectionate hug, which Dev returned awkwardly. "And you must be Ewan. I'm Josh."

"Hi." Ewan offered his hand, and Josh took it, but then he leaned in to kiss Ewan on the cheek anyway.

"It's great to meet you. Rupert didn't tell me you were another redhead. You could almost be brothers!"

Josh looked at Ewan appreciatively, and Ewan flushed at the attention. He and Rupert were quite similar in colouring, although Rupert was taller and considerably more muscular than Ewan.

"Anyway, speaking of Rupert, he's stuck stirring white sauce, so come through to say hi, and I'll get you a drink."

"We brought a bottle." Dev offered the carrier bag containing the wine.

Josh took it. "Great, thanks."

Josh guided them into a large living area with an open-plan kitchen where they found Rupert standing at the cooker, a glass of red wine in one hand as he stirred something in a pan with the other.

"Wow, it smells good in here," Ewan said. "Hi, Rupert."

Josh took Rupert's place at the cooker while Rupert greeted them—shaking Ewan's hand and hugging Dev. Dev looked much more comfortable hugging Rupert than he had Josh, and Ewan fought down a twinge of jealousy. Rupert was only Dev's friend and was quite obviously taken.

"How's that sauce doing?" Rupert put a hand on Josh's hip and leaned in close to look over his shoulder.

"Thickening up nicely." Josh's tone was suggestive, and he turned his head to give Rupert a dirty grin.

"How do you manage to make the most innocent phrases utterly filthy?"

"It's a special skill, babe. You should be used to it by now."

Rupert chuckled and smacked Josh lightly on the arse, then moved away to get a large ovenproof dish out of a cupboard.

A pang of longing flooded Ewan. Not jealousy, but envy for Rupert and Josh and their easy relationship, their togetherness. Just from that small interaction, the love between them was obvious. There were no doubts about what they were to each other.

Ewan's gaze was drawn to Dev. Dev watched them with the same kind of wistfulness written all over his face. Ewan's heart flip-flopped. Was it possible Dev might want the same things he did? Would Ewan screw things up if he asked?

He moved a little closer to Dev, who caught the movement and turned to give him a shy smile. Ewan smiled back, longing to touch him but unsure whether he should.

"Can I get you guys a glass of wine?" Josh asked. Rupert was busily assembling what looked like lasagne. "Or there's beer, or lemonade if you prefer."

"I'll have some wine please," Ewan said.

"Um... me too, thanks." Dev sounded uncertain.

Josh poured out large glasses for each of them and then picked up his own glass from the kitchen counter. It contained something clear and fizzy rather than wine. "Is everything under control here, babe?" he asked Rupert, who was pouring the last bit of white sauce over a layer of pasta.

"Absolutely. Go and chill, I'll join you in a minute. Dinner will be ready in about half an hour."

Josh led them out through large glass doors onto a balcony. "Our garden." He grinned. "It's not very big, but it comes with a view."

"Wow, this is so cool!" Ewan went straight to the railing and looked out over the sea. "You're so lucky to live here."

"It's a definite perk of having a rich boyfriend," Josh said lightly.

Dev came to stand beside Ewan. Ewan resisted the urge to close the gap between them. He had to keep reminding himself that Dev wasn't his to touch, because the urge to put an arm around him or take his hand was strong.

"So, Ewan. You're an undergrad too, yeah? What are you studying?" Josh leaned against the rail on Ewan's other side, a welcome distraction from Ewan's magnetic pull towards Dev.

As Ewan started talking about his course and asking Josh about his, Rupert came outside to join them, and they moved to sit around the balcony table.

They stayed outside to eat, and by the time dinner was served, Ewan was much more relaxed. The wine had filled him with a warm glow and the finer details of his relationship with Dev felt much less important than they had earlier. Josh had put them at their ease by drawing them into conversation. Ewan learned that Josh was in his third year. Despite his finals looming, Josh seemed remarkably chilled.

"Aren't you nervous? I think I'll be shitting myself this time next year."

"I'm staying focused and doing my best." Josh shrugged. "It's all I can do."

"You'll do great," Rupert said reassuringly.

Ewan thought uncomfortably about his own exams that were coming up soon. But he'd worked hard all year and was pretty sure he'd do okay. His only weak spot was statistics, and he was already feeling more confident about that, thanks to Dev.

They fell quiet for a while, all focused on eating rather than talking. The table was small, and Dev sat adjacent to Ewan. Their knees bumped occasionally, and when they weren't in contact, Ewan was acutely aware of the space between them and his desire to close it.

Every now and again, Ewan would catch Dev's gaze on him. Dev's eyes were dark and hard to read behind his glasses, but Ewan thought he saw a softening when their gazes met and held for a few seconds. Dev watching him made Ewan clumsy. Carefully, he picked up his glass and drank, noticing Dev had hardly touched his wine. There was water with the meal too, and Dev was drinking that instead.

After they'd finished the main course, Josh cleared the plates, refusing any offers of help. He returned from the kitchen with a huge tub of ice cream and some bowls and spoons. "I was in charge of dessert, but I cheated and bought ice cream." He grinned.

Rupert huffed, but his lips curved in affectionate amusement. "You always buy ice cream."

"That's because nothing I could make would ever come close to the perfection that is cookie dough ice cream. Does everyone want some?"

Everyone did.

Ewan knew Dev had a sweet tooth, and he wasn't surprised when Dev accepted seconds. Ewan declined and tried not to watch too intently as Dev spooned the ice cream into his mouth, licking his lips occasionally and making appreciative sounds. Ewan shifted in his seat and wondered whether Dev realised he made the exact same sounds when he sucked Ewan's cock. Ewan spread his legs a little to make space for the semi currently swelling in his jeans, and when his knee pressed against Dev's, he didn't pull it away.

Dev didn't move either.

Once, after a particularly prolonged scrutiny of the way Dev wrapped his lips around the spoon, Ewan caught Josh watching him with an amused expression. Cheeks heating, Ewan looked down at his empty bowl, knowing he was being too obvious. The wine was making him careless.

After they'd finished, Rupert and Josh cleared the table and left Dev and Ewan alone for a moment. Ewan's gaze moved inexorably to Dev again, and he found Dev looking back.

The tension was thick, and Ewan was suddenly positive Dev could feel it too. His eyes were huge and dark, and his lips parted slightly. There was a pale smear of ice cream on the lush pink of Dev's lower lip. Ewan's pulse thumped in his ears.

A clatter of crockery came from the kitchen and the sound of Rupert and Josh talking filtered through.

"You've got some…." Ewan lifted his hand and wiped away the ice cream with his thumb. He let his hand linger, his fingertips on the softness of Dev's cheek, skimming lower to catch the hint of stubble on his jaw. Caught up in the beautiful inevitability of the moment, Ewan leaned closer, closing the gap until the caress of Dev's breath became a kiss. Dev's lips parted and their tongues touched. Dev sucked in a sharp breath and put his hand on Ewan's knee, gripping tight as though it was a lifeline.

"Would you like some coffee? Or more wine?" Josh's voice made them spring apart. "Oh, sorry. I didn't mean to interrupt." He grinned at them and explained to Rupert, who was coming through the door behind him. "I just caught them snogging. I guess that means I was right." Then, to Ewan and Dev again. "You're such a cute couple. Don't stop on my account."

Dev's face flushed. Ewan knew his own cheeks must be bright pink too—his fair skin always gave him away. With his brain still lodged somewhere in his groin, Ewan tried to think of an appropriate response because Dev was clearly lost for words.

Thankfully, Rupert broke the excruciating silence. "Oh, stop teasing them, Josh. Now, who wants some coffee or tea?"

"Yes, please," Ewan said. He was feeling light-headed — a combination of too much wine and the tumbling realisation of his feelings for Dev. Josh's words echoed in his head.

You're such a cute couple.

Ewan's heart ached with how much he wanted Josh's assumption to be true. He sneaked a sidelong glance at Dev, whose cheeks were still painted with a blush.

Dev met his gaze and gave him a shy smile before looking away quickly. Hope flared in Ewan's chest.

This has to mean something. I'm not imagining it.

Josh took their orders for tea and coffee, and when he came back with steaming mugs, they sat and looked at the view again.

"It's stunning," Dev said wistfully.

The sun was just disappearing over the horizon and the sky was darkening fast. Josh had pulled his chair next to Rupert's to watch the sunset, and Rupert had his arm around him while Josh snuggled close. Opposite Ewan, Dev pulled up his hood and curled both hands around his cup of tea.

"Are you cold?" Rupert asked him. "We can go inside if you want?"

Dev shook his head. "No. I'm fine." There was a faint smile on his face as he looked out over the inky water, but he shivered slightly, and Ewan wished he could move closer and keep him warm.

When they'd finished their drinks, Josh picked up their mugs and stacked his and Rupert's empty ice cream bowls. "I'll take these in. I'm going to get another layer to put on if we're staying out for a bit."

"Let me help." Ewan picked up the final couple of bowls. Indoors, he put them down on the kitchen counter before asking, "Can I use your toilet?"

"Of course," Josh replied. "It's back out in the hallway, the door next to the front door."

Ewan relieved himself and took his time washing his hands. The light was bright in here, and he stared at his reflection, jaw set.

You need to man up and tell Dev how you feel. If there's a chance he feels the same way, then it's got to be worth it.

He turned off the tap and stood, hands dripping, lost in thought. Their arrangement would be coming to an end soon enough, anyway. He had nothing to lose. If Dev didn't feel the same, the only thing hurt would be his pride. It was time to be honest.

Reaching for the towel, Ewan straightened up and squared his jaw. He was going to do this. He'd say something tonight, when they got back. He'd invite Dev in and tell him he wanted more; he'd ask him out, ask him to be his boyfriend. They were already doing everything boyfriends did together; it wasn't such a big leap. They were good together. Surely Dev could see that too?

Josh was still in the kitchen, stacking things in the dishwasher, as Ewan passed back through the living area. Approaching the doors leading to the balcony, Ewan heard Dev's voice filter through.

"He's not my boyfriend, Rupert. It's not like that."

Ewan stopped in his tracks.

Dev sounded very certain. Too certain. As though it wasn't something he'd even consider. All Ewan's optimism vanished and his heart sank like a stone. He was surprised as well as hurt, because after their kiss earlier, he'd really started to believe that Dev wanted the same things he did.

Not wanting to hear any more, Ewan turned away from the doors.

"Let me give you a hand," he said to Josh, who was still tidying things in the kitchen. "I'll wash up the pans."

"There's no need. I'll do them tomorrow," Josh protested.

But Ewan had already started running water. "It's no trouble, honestly." He needed something to do, a distraction while he tried to squash down his disappointment, ready to face Dev again.

CHAPTER FIFTEEN

"He's not my boyfriend, Rupert. It's not like that."

Even as Dev said the words, disappointment weighed heavy in his chest. He picked unhappily at his fingernails, not wanting to see the kind expression on Rupert's face. Rupert wouldn't understand. How could he? He and Josh were the perfect couple, obviously both on the same page, all settled and happy together.

Dev sighed.

There was a pause before Rupert asked gently, "Do you want him to be your boyfriend?"

Dev shrugged. "It doesn't matter what I want. That's not what this is."

"It could be. Come on, Dev. Josh caught you kissing earlier, and I can tell by the way you look at each other it's more than casual sex."

"It's not that simple." Dev's voice came out tight and snappy; his heart twisted uncomfortably.

"Relationships rarely are."

"This isn't a relationship... well, not in the sense you mean, okay? We're just sort of... friends with benefits, or something like that." His cheeks heated. He didn't want to explain the exact nature of his arrangement with Ewan.

"But you like him."

Dev nodded.

"And you want more?"

Dev took a long breath, his brain ticking over as he considered Rupert's question. *Did* he want more? He and Ewan had an agreement, and Dev had a plan. A relationship with Ewan hadn't been the goal. Ewan was supposed to be a stepping stone on the journey, not the destination.

Dev examined his feelings for Ewan—new, unfamiliar feelings he wasn't sure how to categorise. The physical attraction was undeniable, and he liked Ewan. He was happy when he was with him, and he missed Ewan when they were apart. The pull was strong and getting more powerful by the day.

Is this what falling in love feels like?

"Dev. Do you want it to be more than just a casual thing with Ewan?" Rupert's voice was gentle, but it dragged Dev back from his mental tangent.

"Yes," Dev said. The answer was obvious. "Yes, I think I do."

"Well, then. You should tell him how you feel. The way he watches you when you don't know he's looking… I think there's a chance he might feel the same way."

"Do you really think so?" Dev's heart gave a hopeful little flip and he tried to squash it down. "I'm not sure."

"Yeah. I do."

Dev sighed, remembering the no-strings deal he'd made with Ewan. "But it's complicated. You don't understand."

Rupert snorted. "I understand 'complicated' all too well." His expression was hard to read. There was amusement there, but with a wry edge. "Believe me, Dev. Josh and I wrote the book on complicated. Maybe one day we'll tell you how we met and ended up together, but it's a long story, and it's not all mine to tell. Suffice to say I know all about complicated, and I remember how scary it is to be honest about your feelings. But what's the alternative? You let Ewan carry on thinking this doesn't mean anything and eventually you drift apart? Take it from someone who's been there, if you have feelings for Ewan, tell him. Give it a chance. I know you don't believe he wants more, but he might surprise you."

Dev was silent, absorbing Rupert's words as he stared out at the night sky over the sea. A few stars were visible between the clouds, bright points of light in the darkness. He took a long breath and let it out slowly. "I'll think about it." A cold gust of wind blew and he shivered, hunching into his seat and wishing he had another layer to put on.

"You look freezing. Let's go inside now."

Back in the flat, Ewan was finishing washing up the pans that hadn't fit in the dishwasher. Josh had wiped the surfaces, so the kitchen was spotless and gleaming.

"What do you want to do now?" Rupert asked. "We could play a board game… or maybe cards?"

"What about poker?" Josh suggested. "We don't play for money, just for fun. We've got a set of chips."

Dev looked at Ewan, trying to gauge his interest. It wasn't late, so there was no rush for them to get back. A thrill of nerves and anticipation rippled through him at the thought of being alone with Ewan. He wondered if he'd be able to find the courage to talk to him, as Rupert had advised.

Ewan avoided Dev's gaze. "Yeah, that sounds good."

Dev shrugged. "Okay." He'd played poker before and quite enjoyed it. He was excellent at working out the probabilities of different hands, but he wasn't so good at bluffing or telling when other people were.

They sat around the table in the living area, and Rupert opened a second bottle of wine. Ewan accepted some, but Dev declined. He hadn't finished his wine earlier, and someone had cleared his glass away, so he had lemonade instead, like Josh.

Dev sat opposite Ewan. The game gave him lots of opportunity to study him. But unlike earlier in the evening, Ewan rarely caught Dev's eye, but kept his gaze fixed on his cards most of the time. On the rare occasions their eyes met, Ewan looked away quickly and didn't return Dev's tentative smiles. There was a strange tension about him that Dev didn't understand. Maybe Ewan felt embarrassed about being caught kissing earlier?

Josh turned out to be really good at poker and an expert bluffer. Eventually he had almost all the chips. Rupert and Dev were both out of the game completely, with just Ewan and Josh left in.

Ewan pushed his last few chips to the centre of the table. "I would give you my house keys, but it's only rented." He grinned as Josh pushed in enough chips to match his bet.

Ewan's mood had rebounded to cheerful as the game progressed. Dev suspected it had something to do with the wine that he and Rupert were still drinking.

Ewan changed two cards the first time, and so did Josh. They couldn't raise the stakes because Ewan had nothing left to offer. The second time, Ewan swapped one card while Josh stuck.

"Showtime," Josh said, his face impassive.

Ewan's face spread into a broad smile as he laid out his cards. "Read 'em and weep. Full house, aces on queens."

Josh flipped his cards over. "High straight."

"*No way.*" Ewan leaned forwards to check. He shook his head. "You jammy fucker!" His cheeks were pink and his voice loud.

When Rupert laughed, Dev noticed he was flushed too. The second bottle of wine was nearly empty. That probably accounted for their slightly glazed expressions, but it was good to see Ewan smiling and laughing again after being quiet and withdrawn for a while earlier.

"One more round?" Rupert asked, shuffling the cards.

"Definitely," Ewan said enthusiastically.

Josh glanced at the clock and then caught Dev's eye. Dev shrugged. "Sure."

"Go on, then." Josh leaned back in his chair and stretched, yawning as he addressed the rest of them. "If you think you can take another crushing defeat."

"You're so cocky." Rupert started to deal.

This time it was much closer. Nobody lost all their chips, and although Josh was still doing the best, the others managed to stay in.

The game went on and on. Josh yawned more frequently, and Dev was knackered too. Rupert and Ewan seemed immune to tiredness, intent on the game and enjoying every minute of it.

Finally, Josh said, "I'm sorry, guys, but I'm going to need to duck out. I'm knackered, and I've got a lot of revision planned for tomorrow. But feel free to carry on without me."

"Oh, I'm sorry, babe." Rupert looked contrite. "I hadn't realised how late it was."

"Yes, we should go," Dev said. It was nearly midnight.

Josh and Rupert saw them to the door, and they all exchanged hugs and kisses on the cheek as Ewan and Dev thanked them for dinner.

"The poker was really fun," Ewan said. "Even if you're hard to beat."

"You guys should come over again soon," Josh said. "Maybe you'll have better luck next time."

Ewan glanced at Dev and his smile slipped a little. "Yeah. Maybe."

As the lift carried Ewan and Dev down, an awkward silence filled the space between them.

Dev stared at his shoelaces and wondered what Ewan was thinking. If only people had thought bubbles, like in comics... although maybe not all the time, because that could make life awkward. But sometimes it would be really useful to know what another person was thinking.

"That was a fun evening." Dev finally raised his head to look at Ewan, but the words didn't come out sounding very certain.

The lift came smoothly to a stop and the door slid open.

"Yeah," Ewan agreed as they walked out of the lift. "They're both really cool."

"It was nice to get to know Josh better."

Outside, the air was cold, the sky above mostly clear, and the wind had dropped.

"How long have Rupert and Josh been together?" Ewan asked. "They seem really happy."

"About a year, I think." Dev put his hands in his pockets. He was aching to reach for Ewan, to take his hand. But after Ewan's strange coldness earlier, he was afraid to try. He remembered his conversation with Rupert and wished he had Rupert's confidence in Ewan's interest.

Dev was so confused. The kiss they'd shared on the balcony could make him believe Rupert was right, but then afterwards, Ewan had behaved so differently. Maybe the alcohol had lowered his guard and he now regretted his impulsiveness.

This is why people need thought bubbles.

Dev sighed. They needed to talk. Things weren't right between them. Their previous easy connection had morphed into something tangled and tense. But it was late, and now wasn't the best time. Dev decided he would try and talk to Ewan tomorrow, when he'd had a chance to sleep on it and Ewan had sobered up.

They walked the rest of the way back in uncomfortable silence. Dev wanted to break it, but he didn't know how. Ewan was miles away, his usual easy chatter noticeably absent. When they reached their street, they paused on the pavement.

"Goodnight, then," Dev said miserably. He turned to walk up the steps to his house, but Ewan caught his hand.

"Wait." There was an urgency to his tone that caught Dev's attention.

Dev turned back, and Ewan's face reflected his own unhappiness. "What?"

Dev wanted to go to bed, to wrap his duvet around him, close his eyes, and sleep. Maybe everything would make more sense in the morning, and perhaps then he could find the courage to talk to Ewan and fix whatever was wrong.

Ewan tugged on his hand, pulling him closer. He put his hands on Dev's cheeks and leaned in to close the distance between them, pressing their lips together.

We should be talking, not kissing. But despite Dev's misgivings, his body responded to Ewan's touch. A hopeless wave of longing mingled with desire swept through him, and he put his arms around Ewan and kissed him back. Dev poured all his feelings into the kiss as he clung to Ewan—all the things he couldn't find the words for—and it was as though Ewan was saying them back. The tension in Ewan's hands, the arch of his body against Dev's, the hungry pull of his lips and the thrust of his tongue in Dev's mouth…. It felt real and meaningful, and Dev's heart broke a little at the thought of losing it if Ewan didn't feel the same way he did.

He tried to pull away, but Ewan wouldn't let him.

"Dev," Ewan whispered hoarsely, his lips just millimetres away from another kiss.

His breath was sweet with wine, his hand warm on the nape of Dev's neck where he held him close.

Dev made a helpless sound and fell back into the kiss. Soon they were rocking against each other, hard and desperate. Dev didn't want to come in his pants out there in the street, but he didn't want to stop either. When they kissed like this, nothing else mattered.

Ewan was the one to break the kiss next. Chest heaving as he panted, he stared at Dev in the dim light from the street lamps, his lips wet and his eyes wild.

Dev jerked his head towards his front door. "Do you want to come inside?" He wasn't ready for the night to be over. Every cell in his body craved Ewan, having him was all he could think about. Logic and reason could wait until morning. Was that what obsession felt like? Was it love, or lust? Whatever it was, Dev suddenly understood why people did crazy things in the name of passion. He knew this was a bad idea, knew they needed to talk, but right then he'd take whatever Ewan would give him.

"Yeah." Ewan's voice was a husky croak.

Dev took his hand and they hurried up the steps to Dev's front door.

CHAPTER SIXTEEN

What are you doing?

Ewan's conscience pricked him as Dev fumbled with the keys. He knew this was insanity, but he was past caring.

Dev's words from earlier echoed in his head: *It's not like that.*

Something in Ewan's chest ached. But when Dev was in his arms, kissing him back, none of that mattered.

Dev wants me.

That much was obvious, and right then, Ewan couldn't have stopped himself even if he'd wanted to. He wasn't drunk, but he'd had enough wine to mute his uncertainties and fears. If Dev only wanted him for sex, that was better than nothing, and Ewan would deal with the fallout afterwards.

Ewan followed Dev up the stairs of the silent house, his heart pounding hard. They started kissing as soon as Dev closed the bedroom door behind them, plunging them into darkness.

Ewan gave himself up to the inevitability of it. The kiss contained a sense of urgency he'd never felt in their interactions before, with none of the humour and light-hearted banter Ewan was used to. Their only communication was breathless gasps between kisses and moans of appreciation as they pulled impatiently at each other's clothes.

Ewan toed out of his shoes and pushed Dev's hoodie down his arms, and then they both stripped off their own T-shirts before reconnecting in a messy clash of lips. Ewan groaned at the warmth of Dev's skin against his own, pulling him closer, kissing him harder. He walked back towards the bed, taking Dev with him, and stumbled over something in the darkness. They fell onto the mattress, Dev between Ewan's thighs. Ewan got his hands on Dev's arse, rocking his erection against Dev's hardness.

Ewan gave a grunt of frustration, breaking the kiss to mutter, "Too many fucking clothes."

Dev chuckled. "That's easily fixed."

They rolled to their sides to strip out of their jeans and underwear, and Dev leaned across to turn on the lamp by the bed.

Ewan pulled Dev back on top of him. "That's better. I can see you now." He grinned and Dev smiled back. Ewan lifted Dev's glasses off and set them aside. He slid his fingers into Dev's hair and reeled him in, parting his lips and tasting him again. Dev shifted, and their cocks slid together, hot, silky skin on skin, and Ewan groaned. He clutched at Dev, slipping his hands down to cup his arse, and Dev moved his hips, thrusting against Ewan as though he was fucking him.

"Yeah," Ewan gasped between frantic, desperate kisses. "Fuck, Dev."

Spurred on by Ewan's words, Dev thrust again. The muscles in Dev's buttocks flexed under Ewan's palms. He imagined how Dev must look, on top of him, arse clenching. It must look like Dev was fucking him.

And suddenly Ewan wanted that. He wanted Dev inside him, fucking him, nailing him so hard that he'd feel it tomorrow, as though Dev had left a piece of himself behind.

Dev moaned, and Ewan felt wetness between them. He reached for Dev's cock, smearing the precome over the head with his thumb.

Ewan turned his head to catch his breath, and Dev kissed down his jaw to his throat, licking and sucking as he went.

"I want you to fuck me," Ewan said hoarsely.

Dev froze, his breath warm on Ewan's neck and his body tight with tension.

Ewan's heart hammered against his ribcage as he waited. It felt like forever before Dev spoke.

"What. Now?"

"No, next Friday."

Dev lifted his head and frowned. His dark eyes were glazed and his cheeks flushed. "Huh?"

"Of course *now*." Ewan resisted the urge to roll his eyes. For an intelligent person, Dev could be remarkably obtuse sometimes. "If you want to, of course. Do you?"

"I… uh…." Emotions warred plainly in Dev's features: desire, anxiety, uncertainty. "Fuck yes. I really do." He sounded sure even though he still looked worried. "But are you sure *you* want to? You've been drinking. What if you regret it in the morning?"

"I won't. And I'm not drunk. A little tipsy, maybe, but I know what I'm doing, and I know what I want. I want you—" He kissed Dev's lips lightly to make his point. "—to fuck me." He kissed him again. "Now." Another kiss. "Please?" He gave Dev his most persuasive grin. Nobody could resist that smile. Ewan had used it to devastating effect on other guys and it never failed him.

Apparently, Dev was just as susceptible because his face softened into a smile. "Yeah, okay.

Just… you'll need to tell me what to do. I don't want to mess it up."

"Of course." Ewan liked telling Dev what to do. He was always such a model student. "Get the lube, and a condom."

Dev had to move to reach the drawer, and Ewan missed the warm weight of his body. When he returned to kneel between Ewan's legs, Dev asked, "How do you want to do this?"

Ewan shrugged. "I'm easy. This is your first time. How do you want me?"

Dev bit his lip and flushed. "Like this is good."

"Works for me." Although as Ewan looked at Dev's intense expression, he wondered if doggy-style might make him feel less vulnerable. Ewan was afraid of his face giving too much away.

Dev's hands shook a little and he fumbled with the lube. His nervousness was endearing. Everything about Dev was far too bloody appealing.

Ewan tried not to think about that. Instead he started stroking his cock, which had softened a little during their discussion about whether they were going to do this or not. The grip and slide of his hand soon had him revved up again. His arse clenched in anticipation as Dev rolled on a condom and slicked his cock with lube. Ewan spread his legs and drew them back, offering himself to Dev.

Dev stared at Ewan's arse, mingled fascination and fear on his face. He reached down and stroked his slippery fingers over Ewan's hole. "You look so…."

"Hot?" Ewan suggested.

That earned him a smile. "Yeah. That… but also… I dunno. It just looks so impossible." Dev looked at his dick, and then at where he was stroking tentative circles around Ewan's tight hole. "I mean, I *know* it will work. It just seems like a crazy idea to even try."

Ewan chuckled. "Dev, you've done this to yourself enough times."

"That's different. When it's my arse, I know how it feels, when to push myself and when to be careful. I'm worried about hurting you."

"You won't. For fuck's sake, Dev, I've done this before. I fucked myself with a dildo just last week."

Dev's eyes flew open at that and he licked his lips, gaze flickering between Ewan's arse and his face. "Yeah?"

"Yeah. So will you please just stick your damn fingers in me, and then your cock? Because I'm getting kind of impatient here."

Dev chuckled. "Okay, okay."

He pressed with his fingers at last, and it was Dev rather than Ewan who gasped as the tip of a finger slipped inside.

"That's it." Ewan tightened his hand on his cock, stroking harder as he relished the sensation of Dev's finger in his hole. "More."

Dev frowned in concentration, biting his bottom lip as he gave Ewan more, opening him up carefully until he had two fingers pushed in deep. "Okay?" He met Ewan's gaze.

"More than okay," Ewan managed, his voice a breathy gasp as Dev's fingers skimmed his gland.

Dev watched him carefully, as though he was assessing and cataloguing Ewan's every reaction.

He probably was. Even though this wasn't an official tuition session, Ewan knew Dev would want to learn from this experience — it was who he was. Dev liked to figure out how to do things; he liked to get things right.

"Fuck me now," Ewan gasped. He needed to see Dev lose control, wanted Dev to be desperate like Ewan was, to see that cool scrutiny slip as Dev was swept along with Ewan.

Dev's eyes were huge and dark as he nodded. His blown pupils and flushed cheeks betrayed him — and his cock, of course, hard and thick and sticking out proudly.

Ewan let out a whimper as Dev's fingers slipped free of the grasp of his body, but then Dev's cock was there, skidding over his hole as Dev tried to line it up.

"Sorry," he muttered. "It's not as easy as they make it look in porn, is it?"

Ewan huffed out a laugh, even while his arse ached, clenching desperately on nothing. "Nope." He lifted his legs a little more to help with the angle, reached down too, and their fingers tangled as they got Dev's cock in the right position. "There. That's it…. *Yeah*." His words turned into a moan as Dev breached him. Dev's erection was thicker than his fingers, hot and hard and perfect.

Dev took a sharp intake of breath. His eyes were wide as he stared down at Ewan.

"Good?" Ewan asked.

"Amazing," Dev replied breathlessly, his lips parted.

Ewan was glad they hadn't done it doggy-style. He wouldn't have wanted to miss Dev's expression of wonder.

Dev tightened his grip on Ewan's thighs and thrust forward a little more. It was almost too much, but Ewan didn't want to worry Dev, so he bit down on a hiss of discomfort, knowing it wouldn't hurt for long. Dev withdrew and thrust in again, and that time he dragged over Ewan's prostate, so Ewan's moan was one of pleasure rather than pain.

"Yeah," Ewan gasped. "Like that. So good."

"Yeah?" Dev's hair was messed up by Ewan's hands, and his smile was wide as he fucked into Ewan again and again, lighting Ewan up and sending bolts of pleasure zinging up his spine.

The bed was creaking with a repetitive *thud* as it bumped against the wall. Ewan hoped that whoever had the room next to Dev was a heavy sleeper.

He ran his hands over Dev's torso, feeling the lean muscles flexing under them. "Harder."

"I won't last."

"I don't care." And Ewan didn't care — not much, anyway — because he was close too, and all that mattered was chasing that peak. He needed to come, and just as much as he needed that, he wanted to see Dev come too. He wanted to watch Dev fall apart with his cock inside Ewan, to see Dev's first time fucking someone. A fierce thrill of possession flared in Ewan's chest. He took his cock in hand and started to stroke with purpose. "Yeah, come on. Fuck me, Dev. You're gonna make me come."

The bed banged against the wall harder as Dev gave it his all. He was slick with sweat, the scent of sex strong between them. Pleasure coiled in Ewan's balls, gathering momentum. "Oh yeah…."

And right at that moment, there was a furious banging on the wall.

"Shit... Dani." Dev faltered as though he was going to stop.

Ewan was at the point of no return anyway, and he hoped Dev wasn't far behind. "No! Don't stop." He arched against Dev, squeezing Dev's cock with his arse and trying to keep the rhythm going.

"Shhhhh!" But Dev carried on fucking him despite the interruption, and Ewan was past caring about how noisy they were being.

A few more pumps with his fist and Ewan was coming, crying out and shooting messily over his hand and stomach. Then Dev came too, his lips clamped shut and his face screwed up with the effort of staying quiet. He finally stilled, with his head hanging down as though he was exhausted. Ewan watched, his heart full and a weird lump in his throat.

Finally, as though waking from a trance, Dev came back to earth. He lifted his head and looked at Ewan.

"Hey." Ewan grinned. "You okay?"

"Yeah." Dev blinked at him, as though seeing him for the first time. "Yeah... that was... wow. Sorry I came so quickly. I don't think I'll get any points for stamina."

"I came first," Ewan pointed out. "And it was your first time."

A shy smile spread over Dev's face. "Yeah, that's true." Then his forehead furrowed. "Was it okay for you?"

"Dev. You saw me come, right? It was very okay for me." Ewan reached up and cupped Dev's jaw, drawing him down for a kiss.

The kiss was sweet, but with a delicious edge of dirty that made Ewan's arse tighten reflexively around Dev's cock—which was still pretty hard, considering he'd just come. Dev gasped and jerked back.

"Was that a bit much? Sorry, I couldn't help myself."

"Here, let me…." Dev carefully pulled out and dealt with the condom, passing Ewan some tissues so he could clean the mess off his stomach.

Ewan felt the loss of contact like a limpet torn from its rock. He wanted to keep touching Dev. His libido had been satisfied, but now he craved Dev in a different way. In a much scarier way. Ewan didn't remember ever feeling so needy before. The unwelcome memory of the conversation he'd overheard earlier nudged its way into his consciousness, but he ignored it. The last thing he wanted to do was focus on that now. He was enjoying the illusion of closeness and didn't want to spoil things yet.

He wasn't ready for the night to be over, not unless Dev wanted him to leave.

Dev seemed in no rush to get rid of him. He lay down beside Ewan again and pulled the covers up over them both. He settled into Ewan's arms as though he belonged there, and they kissed some more, gentle, lazy kisses that soothed Ewan's soul. Lying here with Dev, their limbs tangled, sharing breath, he could pretend that Dev belonged to him—that they belonged to each other. It felt so real, so intense, like nothing else mattered.

Eventually the breaks between kissing stretched out, time slowed, and Ewan's heart was a slow thud as his eyelids drooped. Dev yawned, his head on Ewan's chest, Ewan's hand in his hair.

"It's late." Ewan stated the obvious. "Maybe I should go home." Saying the words made his stomach twist. He didn't want to go, but he probably should. Reality would intrude in the cold light of day. Dev wasn't his boyfriend and didn't want to be. Waking up in his bed would only remind Ewan of all the things he wanted and couldn't have.

There was a long silence. Maybe it was Ewan's imagination, but he thought Dev's arms tightened around him as he waited for Dev to respond.

Ewan was just starting to wonder whether Dev had fallen asleep on him, when Dev finally whispered, "Will you stay?"

Ewan's head said no, but his heart screamed yes.

His heart won.

"Okay." He stroked his hand through Dev's hair again and closed his eyes. Maybe it was a stupid idea, but fuck it. One night with Dev was still worth something, even if it was only a fraction of what Ewan wanted.

Dev snuggled closer, one arm thrown warm and heavy across Ewan's torso. With every breath Ewan took, he could feel it there. The reassuring weight was like an anchor.

The seagulls on the roof woke Ewan in the early hours. It was just getting light outside when they started screeching. Ewan usually slept through their racket, but this morning it dragged him into wakefulness. The awareness of warm breath tickling his shoulder and a body in bed beside him startled him. He opened his eyes and blinked sleep away, staring at the ceiling and remembering where he was. He swallowed, his mouth was dry, and a headache born of a little too much red wine throbbed at his temples.

He turned his head to look at Dev lying curled towards him, fast asleep. His lashes were thick, and his shadowed face peaceful and relaxed. Ewan's heart surged as a rush of emotion swamped him. Everything he'd felt for Dev last night was still there, swelling the lump in his throat and making his chest ache.

Why had he been so stupid? When it was obvious he was falling for Dev and that his feelings weren't reciprocated, he should have backed off and kept his distance. Instead he'd done the exact opposite, and he felt a million times worse.

I'm so fucked.

Panic swelled and bloomed, sending out invasive tendrils that tightened in a band around his ribs and stole his breath. He couldn't face an awkward morning after with Dev. The way he was feeling right then, there was no way he'd be able to hide his infatuation. He'd give himself away.

Idiot.

Furious with himself for getting into this situation, he needed to escape, to put some space between them and give himself some time to get over Dev.

He edged away, trying not to let the mattress dip and creak.

Dev stirred and mumbled something but didn't wake. Heart pounding, Ewan stood and gathered up his clothes as quietly as he could. He pulled them on, cursing under his breath as he nearly tripped over Dev's jeans.

When he was dressed, Ewan paused for a few indulgent moments. In the morning sunlight that spilled through the open blind, Dev's hair was a scruffy mess and his olive skin made a lovely contrast to the white sheets. Ewan's heart ached, longing to be back in bed beside him. But he was going to listen to his brain, not his heart—nor his dick. He was going to do the only sensible thing.

Not wanting to be a total arsehole, Ewan paused long enough to scribble a note on the pad on Dev's desk.

Sorry to run out on you, but I woke early and couldn't get back to sleep.

See you soon
E

He stared at the words, guilt pricking him. It was a shitty thing to do to Dev, especially after what they'd done last night. It was cowardly, and Ewan wasn't proud of himself, but he couldn't face Dev that morning. He wasn't ready to have the conversation he needed to have with him, and he needed time to work out how to break off their arrangement as painlessly as possible.

As amazing as last night was, Ewan knew he couldn't do it again. Not when Dev didn't feel the same.

CHAPTER SEVENTEEN

Dev woke feeling gloriously optimistic. A warm pool of contentment filled him, and he smiled into his pillow as he remembered why. After all the confusion and uncertainty of the evening before, Ewan had come back with him and stayed. They hadn't managed to do any talking, but Dev was sure they'd moved past this only being a case of Ewan helping him explore his sexuality.

Last night they'd had sex because they both wanted to, not for any other reason, and it had been amazing. Afterwards, Dev had been afraid Ewan was going to go, but when Dev asked him to stay, he had. Surely that meant something had changed between them.

He stretched, sleepy and comfortable, and then rolled over, wanting to wake Ewan with a kiss… and maybe a blow job.

The disappointment of finding the empty space beside him made Dev's stomach lurch. Hoping Ewan was just in the bathroom, Dev patted the sheets.

They were cold.

He sat up, looking frantically around the room, but Ewan's clothes were no longer scattered carelessly around the floor where he'd abandoned them last night. Ewan was long gone.

The clock told Dev it was almost nine, so not exactly early for a Sunday morning. Maybe there was somewhere Ewan had to be?

Even as he tried to think of all the possible explanations for Ewan abandoning him without saying goodbye, part of Dev's brain was sounding alarm bells and waving warning flags.

Dev might not know much about relationships, but he knew someone running out on you after sex was never a good sign.

But why? Why would Ewan do that?

Nausea swirled in his gut. The only reason Dev could think of was that Ewan regretted it.

They'd broken all their rules last night; having unplanned, non-negotiated sex wasn't part of their deal. Ewan had been drinking last night; he might not have been thinking clearly. God, had Dev taken advantage of him?

He closed his eyes, horror coursing through him.

But no. Ewan might have been a little under the influence, but he had known exactly what he was doing. Ewan had been the one to initiate it with that brain-melting kiss in the street. Ewan had asked Dev to fuck him. Dev would never have expected that, never assumed it was what Ewan wanted. It had all been Ewan's idea. Dev had gone along with it, a more-than-willing participant, but Ewan was the instigator.

So why would he have done such a U-turn this morning? What went wrong?

Guessing was getting him nowhere, so Dev took the direct approach. He got his phone from the pocket of his jeans and texted Ewan, pressing Send before he had time to change his mind.

Where are you? Why did you leave?

It was a few minutes before Ewan replied.

I couldn't sleep. Didn't you find my note?

Hope flickered through Dev. He jumped up, looking around his room until he saw Ewan's scrawl on the pad on his desk.

When he read the words, hope curled up and died. It wasn't a love letter. There wasn't even a kiss or a smiley face. *See you soon*. What did that even mean? Suddenly it was all too clear that something had gone badly wrong between them, but Dev still didn't understand what.

He had to reply to Ewan, but he had no idea what to say.

Got it, he typed and pressed Send, then added *See you soon*, echoing the words in Ewan's note. He wanted to ask *When, when will I see you?* But he was afraid what the answer might be. Perhaps the best thing to do was to let Ewan have some space and wait for Ewan to contact him.

Dev set his phone aside, unhappiness and worry a tight knot in his gut.

When he finally ventured downstairs later in the morning, he found Shawn in the kitchen, frying eggs.

Shawn looked up when Dev entered, and he grunted.

"Hi," Dev said, assuming the grunt was supposed to pass as a greeting. The smell of the hot oil and eggs turned Dev's stomach. He had no appetite. He poured himself some orange juice, chugged it down in a few gulps, and then escaped to the living room.

"Well, hello." Dani smirked at him from where she had curled up on one of the sofas with a book. "You've finally emerged from your sex pit, then.

Where's lover boy? It sounded like you had quite the session last night."

Jez and Mac both turned away from the TV to look at Dev, faces alight with amusement.

"Oh God." Dev cringed, his face heating as he remembered Dani knocking on the wall last night. In all his worry about Ewan's disappearing act, he'd forgotten that part.

"Nice one, Dev," Jez said.

"High five." Mac held out a large hand, which Dev ignored in favour of covering his burning face with his palms as he took a seat beside Dani.

"Yeah... I'm sorry about that." He peeked at her through his fingers. "Did we... uh... wake you up?"

"Yes. I thought your bed was going to come through the wall. At least it didn't go on too long."

Jez snorted. "Nice, Dani. First you embarrass him, and then you insult his prowess."

"I didn't mean it like that!" she protested. "For all I know, there was a long build-up. I just meant the part where the bed was actually banging against the wall didn't go on for hours."

"Not helping!" Dev didn't think it was possible for him to blush any harder. "I'm sorry we woke you up, anyway," he managed.

"So where's Ewan? Have you got him chained up in your sex dungeon?" she asked teasingly.

Dev knew he should try and make light of it, joke back in a way that wouldn't make things awkward, but he didn't have it in him. "No." He swallowed hard, looking down at the carpet. He knew the tone of his voice would give him away. "He left."

There was an uncomfortable silence.

"Is everything okay?"

Jez's voice was kind, and the gentle tone shot like an arrow to Dev's heart. The hurt at Ewan leaving him like he'd done welled up into hot, angry tears that threatened to spill and embarrass him further. He blinked them away and shrugged. "I don't know."

When he dared to lift his head, all their eyes were on him. But the teasing humour had gone, replaced by concern.

"What happened, mate?" Mac asked.

"He stayed over, after we…." Dev waved a hand that he hoped indicated "fucked each other's brains out" or something along those lines. "But when I woke up this morning, he'd already gone."

"Ugh," Dani said sympathetically. "That sucks."

"He left a note," Dev said, "but yeah. It does suck."

"Did you tell him how you feel?" Jez's blue gaze pinned Dev and made it hard to look away. "That you wanted to be more than just fuck buddies or whatever you are?"

"Not yet. I was going to talk to him soon. Maybe I should have done that last night, but it didn't seem like the right time."

Jez frowned. "Maybe he thought he'd overstepped by sleeping over. If you're still only friends with benefits, perhaps he thought it would be awkward in the morning."

"Maybe." That didn't make Dev feel any better about it. He was so sure something had changed between them last night, even though they hadn't talked about it yet.

"When are you seeing him again?" Dani had closed her book, all her attention focused on Dev.

He felt the weight of their concern. It was nice they cared, but it was a little overwhelming. "I don't know. We didn't make any plans."

"You need to talk to him."

"I know." Dev sighed. When had things got so complicated? For a no-strings arrangement, they seemed to have woven a very tangled web. "I will. I'll try and see him later."

Dev left it till the afternoon before getting in touch again. He thought about turning up on Ewan's doorstep, only he was worried he wouldn't be welcome. So he decided to text Ewan and arrange to meet later in the week. When they got together for cooking or tutoring, Dev would talk to him. That would give Dev a little breathing space and time to work out what he wanted to say.

His heart beat fast as he typed.

Want to get together for cooking this week?

He waited a minute or so, but there was no reply. So Dev set his phone down on his desk and went back to the project he had to finish for Thursday. His usual focus deserted him. He doodled idly in the margin, his mind wandering from equations and settling on Ewan again.

When his phone finally pinged, Dev's heart leapt but then sank heavily as he saw what Ewan had replied.

Can't this week, sorry. Too much revision.

Dev knew Ewan had exams coming up. Everyone did. But he still had to eat, didn't he?

Unless he was planning on living on breakfast cereal. But Dev couldn't force him to agree.

Okay. I'll see you Friday as usual then?

After he'd pressed Send, Dev realised there was only one thing left on his list. Bottoming. They'd done everything else. If Dev couldn't find the balls to tell Ewan how he felt, then this Friday would be the last time he got to do anything sexual with him. He really had nothing to lose now.

That knowledge filled him with courage. He was ready to do it. Ready to be honest.

But Ewan didn't reply.

He didn't reply all day, and by Sunday evening, Dev was practically sitting on his hands to stop himself from texting again. He didn't want to be pushy. But why hadn't Ewan got back to him?

He didn't hear anything on Monday either, so on Monday night, Dev texted again.

Hope revision is going well. Will you be okay for Friday? We can run through some stuff for your stats exam.

By the time he went to bed, his phone was still obstinately silent and message-free. Despondent and confused, it took Dev ages to go to sleep that night, and when he did, he dreamed of Ewan's smile and his freckles and his sexy accent.

Ewan lay awake in bed staring at the messages on his phone. He'd read them so many times by now that they were probably seared onto his brain permanently. Guilt gnawed at his gut as he looked at Dev's words—casual, cheerful, expectant. There was nothing there to suggest that Dev felt any differently about him after their night together. It seemed that for Dev, nothing had changed on Saturday night, whereas Ewan's world felt rocked to its foundations.

He ought to reply. Hell, he should have replied on Sunday afternoon. Even if this was just a casual, fuck-buddy thing for Dev, leaving him hanging was still a shitty thing to do. But Ewan had no idea *what* he was supposed to say.

I'm sorry, but I can't shag you anymore because I've gone and fallen in love with you.
Like an idiot.

Ewan snorted and rolled onto his side, phone still clutched in his hand. That would be the most honest answer, but he didn't want to make Dev feel like he owed him anything. Ewan was the one who'd fucked things up by developing these inconvenient feelings. He didn't see the point in admitting them to Dev when Dev didn't want what he wanted. It would only make things awkward between them.

The idea of losing Dev as a friend hurt just as much as losing the sexual side of their relationship. Maybe if Ewan could get through Friday night without giving himself away, then things would come to a natural end and they could transition to friendship?

He squeezed his eyes shut and imagined fucking Dev. His body reacted, surging with arousal, but the emotions that flooded him along with the desire were overwhelming.

He couldn't do it.

He couldn't sleep with Dev again and hide how he felt. He'd do something awful—like cry during sex—and give himself away.

When Ewan opened his eyes and looked at his clock, the numbers showed it was nearly one in the morning. They mocked him, bright and unforgiving.

No sleep for you tonight.

"Fuck it." Ewan got up and pulled on his running shorts and a T-shirt, then sat on the edge of the bed as he put on his trainers. Perhaps a run would clear his head and exhaust him enough so that he could finally sleep.

The city streets were eerily quiet. Ewan set off at a fast pace, his footsteps echoing as he pounded the pavements until his heart raced and his lungs burned. Without consciously thinking about it, he took his usual route: down through the centre and towards the Hoe.

As he ran, his mind emptied. The peace was welcome after hours of ruminating obsessively. When he reached the Hoe, he was greeted by the muted *swoosh* of the sea hitting the rocks along the front. The tide was high with a bit of swell. He ran towards the sound and turned to take the path along the front, passing close to Rupert's flat before looping back along the seafront and over the Hoe. His legs ached, but he pushed himself harder, limbs pumping, breath harsh as he climbed the steep path.

At the top, Ewan stopped to catch his breath. He stared out to sea, remembering how Dev had looked at this view the evening before. His heart flipped. More thoughts of Dev rushed back in, unbidden, filling his consciousness as surely as the waves swept into the rocky coves below.

Panic flooded Ewan. He was in too deep. There was no way he could see Dev on Friday. He was going to have to call it off. But not by text, that was too cruel; face-to-face would be better. Tomorrow he'd go to see Dev and would somehow find the right words to end their arrangement.

With a heavy heart, Ewan turned and started to run again, pushing himself until every cell in his body screamed for mercy. He tried to chase away the pain in his heart with the pain of his body, but he didn't succeed.

By the time he got home, he was so knackered that after a quick shower to rinse off the sweat, he thought he'd finally be able to sleep.

Sure enough, when he fell into bed — and despite the residual ache in his chest — Ewan enjoyed the dreamless rest of the truly exhausted.

"Have you talked to Ewan yet?" Jez asked as they crossed paths in the kitchen on Wednesday morning. Dev was making toast, glaring at the toaster as he waited for it to pop.

"No." Dev sighed. "I'm pretty sure he's avoiding me. He's not replying to my texts."

Jez poured milk over his cereal. "You could go round and see him?"

"Maybe."

But the thought of turning up on Ewan's doorstep was unappealing. If Ewan didn't want to see him, Dev didn't want to force the issue. A cold ball of hurt had lodged in Dev's stomach. Ewan obviously didn't want to spend time with him anymore, and if that was the case, there wasn't much Dev could do to change his mind. All he could salvage from this was his pride, and he wasn't going to beg.

That evening the doorbell rang as Dev was distracting himself by playing *Mario Kart* with Jez and Mac, who were on a break from their revision. "Just one more game," had turned into several, and Dev was only too happy to be swept along with it. It was hard to think about much else when you were trying not to fall off the track on Rainbow Road.

Engaged in a fierce battle for the top three places, none of them moved for the doorbell.

The bell rang again.

"Fuck, isn't anyone else in?" Mac growled, hitting the Pause button.

He hauled his long body off the sofa and went to answer the door.

Dev eased the tension out of his shoulders. He'd been hunched over the controller for far too long.

"Dev?" Mac called from the hallway. "It's Ewan, for you."

Dev's stomach did a peculiar swoop — half anxiety, half excitement. "Sorry. I'll bail on this game," he said to Jez.

"Sure." Jez nodded. "Good luck," he added quietly.

Dev passed Mac in the doorway, who gave him an encouraging smile.

"Hi," Dev greeted Ewan uncertainly.

"Hi."

Ewan made no move to touch him, and a cold hand squeezed Dev's heart. Ewan's freckled face was paler than usual and there were dark smudges under his eyes. His mouth had a pinched, unhappy look to it. Dev might not be the best at non-verbal cues, but even to him it was obvious he wasn't going to like whatever Ewan had to say.

Ewan's next words confirmed Dev's worse suspicions. "We need to talk."

Had four words ever sounded so ominous? "Upstairs?"

Ewan nodded.

Dev led the way, his heart sinking lower with each step. He dragged his heels, trying to delay the inevitable.

As soon as Ewan closed the door behind them, he started talking as if he was desperate to get this over with.

"I'm sorry, Dev. But I can't do Friday. I... I want to call things off."

Even though Dev had seen it coming, the words still struck him like a blow to the solar plexus, robbing his breath. He managed a single word. "Why?"

Ewan's gaze slid away from Dev's and he flushed. "I just... I don't want to carry on with our arrangement. I'm on top of my statistics now, and I think you've learned plenty from me. You don't need me anymore."

"But you never topped me."

The words escaped before Dev could stop them. He was pretty sure Ewan was already well aware of that— the one thing on the list they hadn't done. Knowing it was never going to happen made Dev ache. He hadn't meant to get so attached to Ewan, but maybe it was inevitable. Humans had evolved to bond with people through sex. He should have seen it coming.

It had been stupid to think he'd be able to do all that stuff with Ewan and not care about him. Ewan had been his first for everything—well, almost everything—and that meant something to Dev.

He wanted Ewan to be the first person to fuck him too. "Couldn't we just do that? It's only one more evening. Then we can call it quits. I didn't think fucking me would be too much of a hardship."

So much for not begging. Dev was horrified at himself, but he couldn't help it. One more evening with Ewan would be better than nothing, and if he knew it was the last time, at least he could make the most of it.

Ewan's flush darkened and he frowned. "No. Like I said, I don't want to do it anymore."

His voice was harsh and the words stung like a slap in the face.

"I don't understand." How could Ewan go from wanting Dev to fuck him, to not wanting him at all? "What's changed?"

"It feels like things got out of hand." Ewan's amber gaze bored into Dev's, and there was something there Dev couldn't read, some meaning that eluded him. "It was supposed to be a fuck-buddy thing, friends with benefits… but this weekend was different. I think it's best if we stop before anyone gets hurt."

"Well, maybe it's too late for that," Dev blurted out. His cheeks burned and his eyes stung.

There was a long pause.

"What do you mean?" Ewan's voice was hoarse, and there was tension written in every line of his body.

"I'm sorry." Dev shrugged. "I didn't mean to fall for you. I know this was supposed to be a no-strings arrangement. I thought I could do that, but I can't. I'm sorry I made you uncomfortable by wanting more."

Ewan's eyes widened and his frown melted away. "Wait... what? You like me? *You* want more?"

Dev nodded, feeling pathetic and needy. All his layers were stripped away, and he'd never felt so vulnerable, like a snail without a shell. He clenched his fists, his nails biting into his palms as he waited for Ewan to apologise again and leave him in peace to have a meltdown.

But instead, Ewan took a step towards him, one hand outstretched. "Dev." His voice was choked. "I like you too. That's what this is about. I didn't want to do this anymore because I thought it didn't mean anything to you. But if you feel the same...." He'd closed the gap between them now and he took Dev's hand, uncurling his fist and lacing their fingers together. "Well. That changes everything."

Dev's brain replayed Ewan's words, afraid of the hope that flared, unwilling to believe them. But there was no other way they could be interpreted. "It does?"

"I hope so." Ewan tugged him closer, and Dev went willingly. "What do you want from me, Dev? In an ideal world, what would we be to each other?"

That was an easy question for Dev to answer. "Boyfriends."

Ewan's face split into a smile that made Dev's knees weak. "I'd like that too."

"You're sure?" Dev could hardly believe it.

"One hundred percent. Do you want me to put it in writing?"

Dev laughed. "I don't think I need that. A gentleman's agreement is fine with me."

"Sealed with a kiss?" Ewan suggested.

"Definitely." Dev reached for him, pressing their lips together and wrapping his arms around Ewan until there was no space left between them.

They kissed until they were hard and breathless, and then Dev pulled Ewan down onto the bed and they kissed some more.

Ewan broke away to ask. "Want to seal it with a hand job as well?"

Dev laughed. "Hell yes." Too impatient to undress, they got their cocks out and jerked each other off, panting into each other's mouths and making soft sounds of pleasure and encouragement. Ewan came first, moaning and shuddering, and Dev followed soon after. They carried on kissing, slower now, until finally they separated to grin at each other, fucked out and high on happy hormones.

Ewan licked Dev's come off his fingers, so Dev tried to do the same with Ewan's. He grimaced a little. "It's nicer when it's warm."

Ewan laughed and passed him a tissue instead.

"So, about Friday," Dev said when they'd put their dicks away and were lying cuddled up on top of the duvet. "Are we back on for that now?"

"What? You mean you want me to take your butt virginity?" Ewan gave a put-upon sigh and rolled his eyes. "God. You're going to be such a demanding boyfriend, aren't you?"

" If you don't want to do it, I'm sure I could find someone to help me out on Grindr...."

"Don't you dare! This is all mine." He squeezed Dev's arse, then suddenly looked uncertain. "Well… I hope it is? Do you wanna be exclusive?"

"Yes."

"Phew. In that case I suppose it's my duty to fuck you." He skimmed his hand over Dev's arse, teasing and sending a delicious shiver up Dev's spine.

"Do I have to wait until Friday?" Dev asked hopefully.

"Yes." Ewan sighed. "I have an essay due in on Friday morning, so I'm going to have to go home soon to work on it. I'll be busy with that tomorrow night too. But on Friday, I'm all yours."

"Okay." Dev's mind ticked over with possibilities. He wanted to make Friday special. Their relationship had all been back to front so far. This seemed like an ideal opportunity to start over.

"Right." Ewan pressed a kiss to Dev's cheek before pulling away and sitting on the edge of the bed to put his shoes back on. "I'm really sorry I can't stay."

Dev sat beside him and ran his hand down the curve of Ewan's spine. "Me too. I'll text you about Friday, where and when?"

"Sure."

"And you'd better reply this time," Dev said, a flare of remembered hurt at Ewan ignoring him.

"Yeah. I'm so sorry." Ewan turned and pressed a fierce, determined kiss to Dev's lips. "I'm sorry I hurt you. I was just freaking out when I realised how much I cared… and I didn't think you felt the same."

"I know."

"I was an idiot."

"We both were."

Ewan grinned. "That's why we're perfect for each other." He kissed Dev again, deeper this time, and then groaned as he reluctantly pulled away. "Okay. This essay isn't going to write itself."

He got up, and Dev followed him downstairs to see him out. One final kiss on the doorstep, and then Ewan was gone and Dev was left, missing him already but with a huge smile on his face.

He walked into the living room. The TV was off now, and books and papers lay scattered on the coffee table, evidence of studying. But Jez was sitting in Mac's lap, snogging him like they were about to get down to it on the sofa.

"Whoa. I thought you two were supposed to be revising."

"We are. This is Mac's reward for telling me about the impact of climate change." Jez looked up, his hair messy from Mac's hands and his lips wet from kissing. He clocked the expression on Dev's face. "Did you fix things with Ewan, then? You look like you just won the lottery."

"I feel like it. And yes, we fixed things."

"That's awesome, Dev. Good for you."

"Nice one," Mac agreed, holding out his fist for Dev to bump. His cheeks were flushed and he looked a little glazed.

"I'll, um, let you get on with your *revision*, then." Dev gestured at their books. "Although I think maybe you should take this upstairs, given your revision techniques."

"We will later," Jez assured him. "If I can list all the ways to combat global warming, then I get a blow job, so we'll definitely go elsewhere for that."

Dev chuckled as he left them to it.

CHAPTER EIGHTEEN

The only thing that got Ewan through the next couple of days was the thought of seeing Dev on Friday night. His essay was a tricky one to write, and after scrapping several paragraphs, and rewriting them he was losing the will to live by Thursday evening.

A text from Dev was enough to make him smile.

Can't wait to see you tomorrow. Do you want to come round here? I'll cook you dinner.

Sounds great, Ewan replied. *What time?*

7.30 okay with you?

Sure.

How's the essay going?

Ewan groaned aloud. *Don't ask.*

Oh dear. That bad?

Yeah, but it's nearly done now. Ewan sighed, glaring at the words on his screen. *Just another two thousand words to go.*

Good luck. See you tomorrow.

Thanks. Ewan added a kiss. Because fuck it, Dev was his boyfriend now. He was allowed to be soppy.

He got two kisses and a smiley face back. Ewan grinned. Tempting though it was to carry on this text exchange, the sooner he got this fucking essay done, the sooner he could sleep. He wanted all his energy for tomorrow.

An image of Dev fucking himself on the blue dildo flashed across Ewan's consciousness and his cock took an interest.

"Down, boy," Ewan muttered. Ignoring his semi, he got back to work.

Mac opened the door to Ewan on Friday night, and he broke into a welcoming smile. "Hi, come in."

"Hi."

"He's in the kitchen," Mac said. "There was a cooking crisis, so he couldn't come to the door."

"Sounds ominous. Okay. I'll go and find him."

"Oh, and Ewan?" Mac put a hand on his arm and his voice was earnest. "I'm glad you two worked things out."

"Thanks." Ewan grinned, happiness filling his chest. "Me too."

The kitchen was hot and condensation coated the inside of the windows. Dev was alone in there, stirring something in a pan while another pan hissed on the back burner as it boiled over.

"Need a hand?" Ewan asked.

"No. It's all under control." Dev didn't look up. His arse wiggled as he stirred.

"You might want to turn that back ring down."

"Yes, I've got it. Thanks." Dev spared a hand to do that before starting to stir frantically again.

He obviously couldn't leave what he was cooking, so Ewan went to him. He stood behind Dev and put his hands on his hips. "Hi." He pressed a kiss to the back of Dev's neck.

"Hi." Dev's voice was softer as he turned so Ewan could reach his lips for another brief kiss. Then Dev turned back to his cooking.

Ewan looked over his shoulder. "What are we having?"

"Macaroni cheese. It *sounded* easy."

His disgruntled tone made Ewan chuckle. "It's easy if you buy the sauce, but making it from scratch is a little harder."

"You don't say. It's gone all lumpy." Dev poked at one of the lumps with his spoon, trying to break them up, but it didn't work.

"It'll still taste good. Are you sure I can't help?"

"No. Everything else is done. We're having it with salad, and I've already grated the cheese for the topping. Do you want to help yourself to a drink? I got some beer, or there's lemonade if you prefer. Second shelf down in the fridge."

"Do you want anything?"

"Lemonade, please."

Ewan fetched a can of lemonade for each of them.

Dev's cheeks were pink from exertion and his glasses had steamed up. He looked like he could do with cooling down.

"Can I open a window?" Ewan asked. "It's boiling in here."

"Yes. Please."

Cool air rushed in as Ewan opened the window wide. "That's better."

He kept out of Dev's way as Dev finished cooking. The sauce was pretty lumpy, but once mixed with the macaroni, it wasn't too obvious. Dev put some frozen peas on to boil before pouring the pasta and sauce into an ovenproof dish. He sprinkled a mixture of cheese and what looked like breadcrumbs on the top.

"That looks great."

"It's supposed to make a crispy topping." Dev studied the recipe he'd printed out. "But the breadcrumbs were a bugger to make without a food processor. Okay. Now I just need to put it under the grill for a few minutes, and it will be done."

Once the dish was under the grill and the peas were simmering, Dev grinned, triumphant. "That wasn't so bad."

"Look at you. You'll be on *Masterchef* before you know it." Ewan stepped forward and pulled Dev into his arms. "Now, come here and kiss me properly."

Their lips met, and Ewan closed his eyes and lost himself in the sensation of Dev. He tasted of sweet lemonade and his hair was soft under Ewan's hands. It felt so good kissing him now that Ewan knew it meant something. The attraction had always been there on both sides, but admitting their feelings for each other took things to a whole new level. The kiss was intense, and although it was arousing, it was also so much more, with a tenderness to it that made Ewan's heart swell along with his dick. He lost all track of time in the slow press of lips and glide of tongues.

The scent of burning pulled him sharply back to reality and he broke away. "Shit. Dev. The dinner!"

Smoke was pouring out from under the grill. It was a miracle the smoke alarm hadn't gone off.

Dev ran to turn off the grill while Ewan opened the window even wider. He turned to see Dev putting the charred remains of the mac and cheese down on the kitchen surface. "Bollocks." He shook his head sadly. "I'm not sure it's going to be edible."

The cheese and breadcrumb layer was black and still smoking, and the smell of burning cheese was disgusting.

"I'm sorry. I distracted you."

"It's my fault. I should have set a timer. Ugh. I'm an idiot."

"You're not an idiot. It could happen to anyone. Anyway, I reckon we can still eat the pasta if we scrape off the topping."

"Maybe." Dev didn't look convinced.

They dished up and carried their plates through to the living room. Shawn and Mike were in the living room playing *GTA*. Mike greeted them amicably, but Shawn barely acknowledged their presence other than to mutter a quick hi. He didn't look up from the game.

Ewan and Dev sat at the table in the window to eat. The pasta and sauce was edible, but it was very bland without the extra cheese from the burned topping. Ewan didn't want Dev to feel worse than he already did, so he tried to look enthusiastic. At least the salad was nice. Dev mostly just pushed his food around the plate and didn't seem to put much of it in his mouth.

After a particularly loud volley of gunfire and swearing, Dev raised his eyes to Ewan's and grimaced. "Want to eat in my room instead?"

"I think I'm done with eating." Ewan pushed his plate away. "Sorry," he added as Dev's face fell.

"Yeah. It wasn't very good." Dev sighed.

Ewan lowered his voice to a whisper. "But I can think of other things we could do in your room."

Dev's cheeks went pink. "Yeah. Me too."

They dumped their plates in the kitchen and left the clearing up for later.

Upstairs, Dev locked his bedroom door behind them. "Well, that pretty much sucked for a first date. I totally messed up the dinner and then we had to eat it to a soundtrack of *GTA* with Shawn and Mike for company, which was probably the least romantic setting ever."

"Hey. The date isn't over yet." Ewan let his gaze rake over Dev as Dev crossed the room to where Ewan stood by the bed. "I think we can still redeem it."

Dev smiled. "That's true."

"So how about you get over here and let me fuck you."

Heat flared in Dev's eyes. "Yeah."

They kept getting distracted by kisses as they helped each other out of their clothes, but eventually they were both naked. Dev dropped to his knees to suck Ewan's cock for a while. He still had his glasses on, and Ewan found it ridiculously hot the way Dev glanced up at him through the thick frames, checking his reaction as he hollowed his cheeks and took him deep.

When Ewan started to get a little too close to orgasm for comfort, he got Dev to lie down on the bed so he could return the favour. Ewan blew him and stroked his hole with spit-slick fingers until Dev was moaning and asking for more.

"Turn over," Ewan said. "I want to eat your arse."

Dev didn't hesitate, flipping onto all fours. "Like this?"

"Perfect." Ewan nosed into his crack, smelling soap and the musky scent of Dev beneath. He reached one hand between Dev's legs to find his heavy cock and stroked it as he licked the tender skin.

"Fuck," Dev breathed. Ewan felt the muscles relax some more. "I'm ready, Ewan. Fuck me."

Maybe Dev was ready, but Ewan was enjoying the rimming too much to cut it short, so he carried on teasing Dev for a while, opening him up with his tongue, and then his fingers until Dev was thrusting back on his hand. "Please, Ewan. Stop teasing!"

"Shhhhh." Ewan squeezed his balls lightly. "Or you'll have Dani banging on the wall again."

"She's away this weekend. Now will you please just fuck me!"

"You're so cute when you're impatient."

"You're a horrible boyfriend."

Dev clenched his arse around Ewan's fingers. The tight squeeze felt way too good for Ewan to resist any longer. He needed that around his cock.

Ewan chuckled. "No I'm not. I'll take care of you."

Dev stayed where he was as Ewan put a condom on and slicked lube over his erection. The sight of Dev waiting like that on his hands and knees, his arse exposed, made Ewan's balls tighten. "You want me to fuck you like this?"

"Yeah." Dev's voice was tight. "I always imagined it this way for our first time. I don't know why."

"Did you think about it a lot?" Ewan moved in behind Dev, using his hand to rub the head of his cock teasingly back and forth over Dev's hole.

Dev's voice was rough as he replied. "If every time I jerked off for the last few weeks is a lot... then, yes."

"Fuck." Ewan lined up and pushed in carefully. Dev was hot and tight and perfect, and he opened up for Ewan as though Ewan belonged inside him. Ewan paused for a moment to let Dev adjust before asking, "You okay? Ready for more?"

"Yes." Dev pushed back greedily, and Ewan groaned as he sank in, balls-deep. Thank God Dev had lots of practice with a dildo, because Ewan found it hard to take things slowly. Dev felt so fucking good.

Ewan started to move. He tried to be careful at first, but Dev encouraged him. "That's so good. Harder—Do it harder."

Ewan was only too happy to oblige. He gripped Dev's hips and went faster, thrusting in deep with every stroke. Abandoned to sensation, Ewan lost track of time. All he cared about was the hot pressure of Dev's body around his cock, the scent of their sweat, the sounds of pleasure that escaped them. Dev dropped forwards onto one elbow, reaching down with other hand to stroke himself. "I'm getting close," he bit out.

"Yeah. Come on." Ewan fucked him harder. "Wanna feel you come on my cock."

Dev moaned, his arm working furiously. He paused for a moment to spit in his palm before carrying on. The slick sounds of his hand drove Ewan closer. He bit his lip, trying to fight his own orgasm, wanting Dev to get there first.

And then he felt it, the pulse of Dev's body as he cried out and started to come. Ewan followed him almost immediately, thrusting deep and grinding his hips as he emptied himself into the condom, into Dev, blinding pleasure overwhelming his senses.

Afterwards, he leaned forward, kissing Dev's shoulders and the back of his neck as he reached around with one hand to gently stroke Dev's cock where it was wet and beginning to soften.

Dev moaned, squeezing reflexively around Ewan one last time, the echo of his climax rippling through him. "That was amazing," he said dreamily.

"Good." Ewan felt his cock begin to slip out, so he pushed himself up and off Dev and tied off the condom before dropping it on the floor. Dev rolled over and lay on his back, looking up at Ewan with easy, open affection.

Ewan flopped down beside him and pulled the covers up. "Was it how you expected? Your first time?"

"It was better." Dev rolled to face Ewan. His expression was soft, and a smile lurked at the corners of his lips.

"How?"

"Because when I planned on getting experience, it was going to be just that. Sex without feelings. I'm sure it would still have been fun. But this is definitely better."

Ewan kissed him on the lips. "Yeah. I think so too." His stomach rumbled. "Sorry. I think I worked up an appetite."

"Well, you didn't eat very much earlier. Do you want to go back down and we can try and make something else?"

"No. I want to stay naked in bed with you." Ewan pulled him closer and kissed him again. But his stomach growled, louder this time. "But I guess more food might be good. How about we order pizza?"

Dev's eyes lit up. "Great idea. I've got the local place bookmarked, hang on."

He fetched his laptop from the desk and they sat side-by-side in bed, arguing about pizza toppings before deciding to just get a pizza each.

"I've picked mine, and now I need to pee, so you order whatever you want. I've got cash, so we can pay when they deliver."

Dev slid the laptop onto Ewan's knee and climbed out of bed. He pulled on a pair of boxers but nothing else. Ewan looked up to admire Dev's tight little arse and long slim legs as he walked towards the bedroom door.

Ewan settled on ham and mushroom toppings and placed the order. As he went to close the window, he must have accidentally swiped something on the trackpad, because Dev's reminders opened. The list that came up was titled *Things to Do This Term*.

There was only one item left on the list:
Find a boyfriend

Ewan frowned. Surely that should be crossed off by now. At the top of the page were five completed items with a link. Knowing he shouldn't be so nosey but unable to resist, Ewan clicked on it. He smiled as he read down the list of things Dev had checked off.

Make some friends
Learn to cook
Research sex stuff
Join Grindr
Get some experience

He heard the sound of water rushing through pipes as the toilet flushed. Knowing Dev would be back any minute, Ewan quickly marked *Find a boyfriend* as complete, and added *Give my new boyfriend the blow job of his life*.

When he heard Dev coming, he left the laptop open on Dev's side of the bed and lay back down with his hands behind his head, trying to look innocent.

"All done?" Dev asked as he came back in.

"Mm-hmm." Ewan tried to suppress a smile.

Dev shed his boxers and approached the bed. His gaze took in the open laptop and what was on the screen. "Hey. What are you doing in my lists?"

"Just making a few small changes. You forgot to tick off one very important one, and I added a new item for you."

Dev lifted the laptop so he could read what was on the screen. He narrowed his eyes and turned a glare on Ewan, but his lips twitched, giving him away. "The blow job of your life, huh? No pressure there."

"I'm sure you can manage it after all that experience you've been getting."

"Oh, I don't know. I think I still need to work on my skills."

"Practice makes perfect," Ewan said. "And there's no time like the present. We've got half an hour before the pizza gets here."

Dev put the laptop down and pounced. Straddling Ewan, he pinned Ewan's hands to the pillows and kissed him hard before sliding down his body and giving him a wicked grin. "Well, I'd better get on with it, then."

EPILOGUE

A few weeks later

Dev gazed at the sunset and took a sip of his lemonade. With Ewan's arm around him, he was comfortable despite the sea breeze and the fact that he'd left his hoodie in the living room. Being with Ewan warmed Dev from the inside out. Surrounded by friends, with Ewan beside him, contentment filled him.

"So, what are your plans for next year?" Ewan asked Josh. "I assume you're sticking around in Plymouth like these two?" He gestured to Mac and Jez who sat opposite, holding hands and looking relaxed and happy.

They were sitting out on Rupert's balcony, with empty Chinese takeaway containers and bottles spread out on the table in front of them. It was a perfect way to celebrate the end of exam season for all of them—except Rupert, as the only non-student amongst them.

Dev's exams had gone pretty well. He hadn't got his results yet, but he was feeling confident. Ewan was less certain, but Dev thought that was just him worrying. He knew Ewan had worked hard. They'd revised together, using some of Mac and Jez's revision techniques—blow jobs were very motivating.

Of all of them, this year mattered most for the three who had done their finals: Josh, Mac, and Jez.

"I've got a few interviews coming up," Josh replied. "One for the finance team at the university, one with a youth charity, and one for a bank. They're all local. Hopefully one of those will work out—subject to me passing, of course."

"If not, you can be Rupert's houseboy." Jez grinned at him. "I'm sure he won't mind."

Josh flipped him the finger. He cast a sidelong glance at Rupert, who was sitting beside him, his hand on Josh's knee. "Yeah, I think he'd live with it. But I'd rather be independent, thanks."

Rupert gazed at him, pride and affection on his face. "You're going to get a first, I'm sure of it. And you'll have your pick of those jobs."

Josh shrugged, but he didn't deny it.

"It must be nice to be so confident." Mac sighed. "I'm a nervous wreck waiting to find out how I did. I'm hoping for a 2:1, but I'm not sure I'll manage it."

"You'll be fine." Jez squeezed his hand. "I have faith."

"Well, if I don't do well enough to go on to do teacher training, I'll have to be *your* houseboy."

"I could go for that," Jez said thoughtfully. "You'd look great in one of those skimpy little aprons that just covers your cock and not much else."

Everyone laughed.

Ewan's arm tightened around Dev. "I'm glad I've got another year before I have to worry about finding a job. I'm not ready for adulting yet."

"What are you guys doing this summer?" Rupert addressed them. "Are you staying in Plymouth or going back home?"

"A bit of both," Dev replied. "Ewan's coming with me to visit my parents, and then we're going up to Edinburgh so I can meet his family." His stomach flipped with nerves at the thought.

"Oh, scary stuff," Jez said. "I was shitting myself about meeting Mac's family. It was okay in the end, though," he added when Dev's face must have registered his anxiety.

"They're going to love you," Ewan said to Dev. "How could they not?"

Dev turned and lost himself in Ewan's smile. They stared at each other, and the rest of the world dropped away for a moment.

"You two are so fucking adorable it's ridiculous." Jez's voice made Dev flush and turn back to the table. All the others were grinning at them.

"Stop pretending to be a cynic," Mac said. "Being in love is awesome, and you should know."

Dev's heart somersaulted. Although he knew he was completely head-over-heels crazy for Ewan, he hadn't said it in so many words yet, and nor had Ewan.

Ewan tightened his arm around Dev's shoulders. "Yeah, it really is." He sounded so certain, so matter-of-fact about it.

"Yeah," Dev managed. It came out a little wobbly because of the lump in his throat. "It's the best."

"To falling in love." Mac raised his bottle of beer.

"I'll drink to that." Josh lifted his lemonade.

"And more importantly, to staying in love." Jez lifted Mac's hand, kissed it dramatically, and then raised his bottle, too.

They all clinked their glasses and bottles together, smiling and laughing.

Dev glanced sideways at Ewan and grinned. He didn't think staying in love with Ewan was going to be too much of a challenge.

About the Author

Jay lives just outside Bristol in the West of England, with her husband, two children, and two cats. Jay comes from a family of writers, but she always used to believe that the gene for fiction writing had passed her by. She spent years only ever writing emails, articles, or website content.

One day, she decided to try and write a short story—just to see if she could—and found it rather addictive. She hasn't stopped writing since.

Connect with Jay

www.jaynorthcote.com
Twitter: @Jay_Northcote
Facebook: Jay Northcote Fiction

More from Jay Northcote

Novels and Novellas
Cold Feet
Nothing Serious
Nothing Special
Nothing Ventured
Not Just Friends
Passing Through
The Little Things
The Dating Game – Owen & Nathan #1
The Marrying Kind – Owen & Nathan #2
Helping Hand – Housemates #1
Like a Lover – Housemates #2
What Happens at Christmas
The Law of Attraction
Imperfect Harmony

Short Stories (ebook only)
Top Me Maybe?
All Man

Free Reads (ebook only)
Coming Home
First Class Package

Jay also has several titles available in audiobook via Audible, Amazon or Apple.

Made in the USA
Charleston, SC
30 June 2016